Michael James Rogers Jr.

SCARE RECORD

AUSTIN MACAULEY PUBLISHERS

LONDON * CAMBRIDGE * NEW YORK * SHARJAH

Ordering Information:
Quantity sales: special discounts are available on quantity purchases by corporations, associations, and others. For details, contact the publisher at the address below.

Publisher's Cataloguing-in-Publication data
Rogers Jr. Michael James
Scare Record

ISBN 9781643789767 (Paperback)
ISBN 9781643789774 (Hardback)
ISBN 9781645365808 (ePub e-book)

Library of Congress Control Number: 2024901444

www.austinmacauley.com/us

First Published 2025
Austin Macauley Publishers LLC
40 Wall Street, 33rd floor, Suite 3302
New York, NY 10005
USA

mail-usa@austinmacauley.com
+1 (646) 5125767

I would like to acknowledge Robert E. Howard, whose descriptive writing style and ability to relate to his characters first made me want to write, and Howard Phillips Lovecraft, who has enriched the future of writers worldwide but also sought to enrich the other writers of his time.

Prologue

I found the record in an old chest of comic books when I was thirteen. I was an avid collector for years, by then, making regular forays to the local card shop on my bike.

It was 1994. The attic was like an endless cave of moldy odds and ends from long lost eras. Old furniture fought for space among wardrobes filled with dated garments. There were cobwebs everywhere, just like in the movies. Five generations had inhabited that house, and the collection of eccentricities must have accumulated for over a century. I never saw the far end of it.

The chest should have been more recent, though, being towards the front. It could have only been there for about twenty years. I thought it was my father's.

I was a teenager now. It was not in me to run and announce my discoveries. That brought with it the chance of things being forbidden. I was a monster-loving sort with stodgy parents. I already knew the lack of welcome anything I had to show them would get—even good grades.

My father wasn't the least bit interested in monsters and comic book heroes. He always asked me what I saw in that 'crap.'

I remember Pop always seemed angry about the subject. He was more than just disapproving. It never occurred to me that he could've been afraid.

I thought it was his chest. He never told me he had a brother. When he finally related the particulars of that tragedy, it was many years too late.

How could I have known? What else would I have done? The contents of that treasure were irresistible. Just look at all those golden era comics. They were worth a fortune! All the cheap and hard to find novelties! I was in Marvel heaven.

I decided to savor the comics later, occupying myself with the x-ray specs and the goofy joy buzzer. How much enjoyment could I get from the fake vomit or the doggy doo? I was shuddering just at the thought of the looks on my parents' faces.

I delved through the layer of gags and came upon the plain white sleeve of a miniature vinyl record.

The circular label glued to it was also white. It featured a nastily drawn face of some hooded creature with its claw outstretched. The big block letters at the top read "GAYLE HOUSE." The lower edge proclaimed it as "The Haunting."

Other less interesting information was also present. 33 1/3 rpm meant something, at least. I glossed over things a lot at that age.

My focus was on the old, children's record player that sat close by. I remember how the thickness of the dust on it was the same as the coating on the chest. I was certain it was from the same fossil layer.

You'd be more likely to listen to a cassette tape or compact disc back then. I could just imagine placing this on my dad's turntable. Like I'd dare touch his fine stereo system. That would definitely be off-limits, messing with his pride and joy. Classical music and the Four Lettermen records would only ever emanate from those four-foot speakers.

Well, I never heard him play the Four Lettermen, but there were more than four albums of them in his lame record collection. Iron Maiden or Boston, now those were records. I would have bought a Yes record just for the cover, but I was more likely to record CDs onto a cassette and listen to it on my Walkman.

No, I had decided that tiny little record was meant to be played on that tiny little box, and I flipped it open to inspect its dusty little needle.

I sat in the attic. A fractured mirror was propped up against a dresser to one side. I wasn't able to see very far into it. It was so grimy you could barely see any reflection at all.

There I was, surrounded by the detritus of ages. I was, kind of, in a trance. I placed the record over the little nub and put the needle on the record.

As I searched for an outlet to plug into, the tiny speaker crackled with noise. A chill went down my spine. My ears were assaulted by the ancient record's sounds. It began with the agonizing groan of a spooky, creaking door.

Through the crispy slurp—slurp of the needle plowing through its' imperfections could be heard faintly clinking chains. Was that someone dragging their foot?

It was supposed to sound like someone limping into the room. I could barely hear the moaning. Something moved over my shoulder. I turned to look, and the record stopped.

A cold chill ran down my back and churned in my guts.

I faced that grimy mirror. It towered over me in its decay. I couldn't be sure I was looking at myself through all that filth.

I don't know why but I took off the record, put it in its sleeve, and closed the box. I thought only of getting out of that scary old attic. I could listen to the whole record in the safety of my room.

Maybe I'd plug it in this time.

I grabbed a few choice comics and closed the trunk on my indiscretions as quickly as I shut the door on my way, the hell, out of there.

I had no idea why but I felt like I needed to leave in a hurry.

My parents were going out that evening. I figured it would be cool to listen to this record late at night. It would make it real spooky.

The posters of Frankenstein and the Creature from the Black Lagoon greeted me as I entered my room. I turned on the lamp by the nightstand and put the stack of plunder under my bed. I would pull out that record after my parents left and put it on the big stereo in the living room.

There was a good monster movie on when mom and dad were preparing to leave. I was reading the old comics I had found, forcing myself to be patient.

I came across the original ad for the scare record halfway through the first issue of Weird War Tales. That had made looking forward to the whole experience that much juicier!

The night was dark beyond the sliding glass door in the living room. There was me, lit by the television's light. Cast in gloom, the couches and surroundings were reflected clearly on the half of the glass door that always remained closed.

I could hear crickets through the screen door and the sighing of the wind through the trees. They rumbled like an ocean tide.

I turned on the stereo. LED's flickered on across its data bank like face. The stacks of its components lay like patient slabs of Mayan machinery winking at me as I closed the glass door.

Seeing my reflection staring back at me, I crouched in front of the cabinet's faint glare. I could see in it the room reflected in the back door behind me. A wall length copy loomed over my back. Everything was directly across from their opposite as reflections have a natural tendency to do.

When you're in motion, your eyes are focused on what you are doing. All your surroundings are blurred out of the corners of your eyes. Everything is taken for granted. That's one of the biproducts of Reality.

Anything out of the ordinary is impossible. You are the only one here, right? Something affected here can be done by nobody other than yourself. You're in charge. You're all alone in the house.

All of this was a given. None of it consciously registered as I rocked back on my heels to bounce my way up from my stooped position, I was just about to push up, when I could see something was standing up at the same time right behind me.

The reflection in the glass had shown someone was, clearly, there. It was already inside the door, with me in the room.

I jumped up and turned around rather more dramatically than intended with the resultant loss of visibility. I looked around. The room was empty.

The shrill, reedy, tone of the crickets took that moment to die out and I was thrust into a world of silence. I just stood there frozen on the spot, chilling sensations flooding down from my head to my toes.

It was terrifying. I thought I just saw the boogeyman! Something was just about to lunge at me out of the corner of my eye. What had thrown that brief reflection?

I took a few deep breaths to settle my nerves.

After making sure the room was all clear I returned to the main highlight of my night: The Gayle House Haunting.

I'd read the ad over and over. "Invite your friends over for a…Haunting" it commanded in big, red balloon letters, "with this haunted sound effects record."

Draped in a spectral sheet, the face of a leering, blue demon roared in silence from the picture's corner, claw outstretched beseechingly like "Give me blood!"

The tutorial continued beneath a rough depiction of a dilapidated house lit by a papery full moon. Through a skeletal tree the moonlight shone as only antique wood pulp and cheap ink could deliver.

"Just imagine how scared your friends will be when you flip out the light" the ad offered, "and they start hearing creepy sounds like the howl of a wolf, a creaking door, chains rattling, and then a man's voice telling them that the house is haunted and they are to die—one by one."

The tortured script blared its ominous offer from a yellow background that could make your eyes bleed.

"They'll be scared stiff when they hear footsteps coming across the floor, the sound of people fighting, glass breaking, hideous laughter, terrible shrieks and screams, eerie moaning and then more footsteps, more screams..." My goodness! "Each person in the room will think that he is going to be the next victim." Yeah. Right.

It then explained how "This 7 inch, long playing 33 1/3 RPM special haunted house sound effects record can be yours for only"—more red balloon letters—"$1.00 (+25 cents for postage and handling)"

It actually claimed "Satisfaction guaranteed or your money back." It was right there above the sectioned off space.

You could tell it was for cutting out and sending away for the record. It was cordoned off by those tiny little dashes.

"THE GAYLE HOUSE" the address read, " Dept H2. P.O. Box 512, Flushing, New York 11352 (Please Print)" followed by the lines for your name, address, etc. etc. "DON'T DELAY. USE THIS RUSH COUPON TO ORDER TODAY!" The blue floating arrow said.

"Be the first in your neighborhood to get this record and invite your friends over for a Haunting!" it repeated in pathetic red. This thing was going to be such a stinker.

Under the reaching, ghoul shone a fine little illustration of a plastic record and tiny letters listing its contents.

"Side 1: The Haunting."
"Side 2: Assorted creepy sounds to be played when the lights are out!"

I picked up the plastic disc in its dirty white sleeve. The same contents were listed on it. Besides the elaborate and colorful album collection, this creased up offering was disappointingly blank. It was a stark white. Well, it did only cost a dollar after all.

I guess all the instructions were in the ad. Like all cheap novelty mail orders in the business, I expected the ad had already provided more entertainment than the product would ever have to offer.

Cheesy. It's gonna be cheesy and lame and poorly done. I mean, just look at the last sentence. "This record creates a real atmosphere of terror with sounds that can almost be seen!" Oh, for sure.

So why was he so freaked out? What charged the atmosphere with such a chilling storm of expectancy?

The crickets outside the half-opened screen door had completely stopped. I couldn't say when. There was no sound of the wind rushing through the trees.

The breeze had totally ceased. I could barely hear the soft roaring of the highway traffic down the road. It usually moaned slowly between our houses and the interstate. Now, the source of that constant background noise seemed especially muffled. I felt like the whole house was trapped in a bubble that ended just at the yard's boundaries. The air began to stale.

The automated arm carried the needle over to the abbreviated plastic disc spinning lazily on the huge turntable.

The crackling sounds of the record had been decreased greatly by the cleaning I had given it with dad's products. A fresh stylus had helped, too. The rhythm of one remaining flaw scritched monotonously in the gigantic speakers. It was a mechanical heartbeat, regular and familiar. It should have reassured me, but it felt more like an approaching storm as the record began.

There it was again—the drawn-out groan of the mother of all creaky doors. Colossal and echoing, it squealed on longer than it was necessary. Then the shuffling gait. By the time the narrator's voice started, I had determined for myself I was safely alone and sat back in dad's big sofa chair content.

"Do not be afraid." A badly acted voice groaned. "I have come from the world of the unliving to warn you. This place is haunted by a Blood Banshee!"

"If you do not leave at once, each of you will die one… by…one."

What followed was a miserable sound like someone doing a wounded moose call through an empty toilet paper roll.

"It's too late," the narrator, a ghost guide perhaps, said dramatically, "the banshee is already here. You are DOOMED."

Then the fruitcake faded off to safety.

"I must GO now. I must go. I must go."

I'd never heard of a Blood Banshee. I had prided myself on knowing about all the monsters. Even Dungeons and Dragons never ever mentioned a blood banshee.

Banshees were well known. They were the spectral washerwomen of some Irish family's ancestors. By all reports, they exist to herald the next death in the family.

This thing, whatever they claimed it was, sounded big and beastly. Its' groan was pathetic. It stomped onto the soundtrack to the noise of one heavy boot being slapped onto the floor.

"Clop…"

"Clop…"

"Clop…"

"IT'S IN THE ROOM!" a boy cried.

More footsteps. More moose calls. It didn't sound like it was hard to outrun. Sure enough, the kid got caught.

"No, please. Let go of my arm. Please. PLEASE!" followed by sounds of commotion that sounded nothing more than a sound effects man rubbing a wooden chair around on the floor.

A few seconds of this and the kid was done for. He let out two short screams and then the most hilarious sounds I had ever heard recorded.

More clear than anything else before it, the sound effects man had put the mike right to his lips. The sipping noises he was making were, positively, juvenile.

"Hueeyoo, hueeyoo, sip sip sip!"

I burst out laughing. This was grand! How could anyone be scared by this?

It was as childlike as the booger ghost story—"I've gotch you where I want you, and now I'm gonna eatch you!" or Bloody Fingers. Stories we'd tell each other in the closet when we were, what, five?

Well, this did fit that era. As sophisticated as Laverne and Shirley.

Ever so slowly, the monster continued its rampage. It went after another boy, howling its miserable sounding call.

"It's not gonna get me! I'm gettin' outta here!" the other boy proclaimed. I guess he wasn't fast enough either.

"NO! Somebody HELP me! I don't WANNA die!"

Again with the chair, scrabbling it back and forth. This time the sound effects guy threw in a couple of glasses, shattering them for good measure.

"No. No…AAAAAH AAAAH!" This boy screamed twice, too. Then the close up sipping and lip-smacking, again.

Suddenly, the tortured hinges of the ancient door were back. It was the only thing to elicit a true picture in my mind on the whole recording. With it came the terribly overdramatized narrator.

"I have returned to DESTROY this evil creature!" he warbled. "With this STAKE, I will END THE CURSE of this demon FOREVER!!!"

The creature's only reply was to repeat itself. It was the only sound it seemed able to make. "Hrooooo! HarooOoo!!"

A different sound rang out. The special effects man had gone for broke and started hammering a windowpane.

'CRISH, CRISH, CRASH'

It was explained by a man's voice. "It's TRYING to GET OUT the WINDOW!" he yelled.

A two chair tussle ensued. The sound effects man must have had one in each hand as someone smashed bottles of glass over his head.

Then came the best line yet. "The STAKE! The STAKE! Give me STAKE!!!"

They must have had the thing pinned because all it could do was continue to moan. This time, it seemed more in pain as the sound effects man smacked a piece of wood against a baseball bat.

Plonk! "HarooOoo!"—once

Plonk! "HarOOOOO!"—twice

Plonk! "Harooooo!"—the thing was sounding tired now.

Plonk! the fourth shot, and it was done.

Then the narrator dragged himself over to get the last word in. Apparently, he had been mortally wounded himself.

"Its days of evil are OVER!" his pompous voice stated. "the BLOOD BANSHEE is dead."

"Uuuuuugh"

With that groan, he expired along with the time left on that side of the record. It ended with a final hiss and pop of the needle.

I stood up and looked at it spinning on the turntable. I lifted it off and held it, just looking at it. I didn't know whether to laugh or cry. At least I didn't waste a dollar twenty-five on it.

It was everything, everything awful that is, I had expected of it. There was a charm to it that made you want to play it again and again. I flipped it over in my hands and set it back on for side two.

As the automated arm carried the stylus over to the edge of the record, I noticed the crickets had stopped again.

On the wall, to my right, was a picture under glass. In its glare was the reflection of the table lamp in the back door. What I saw after the needle set down made me turn and wish there was room to back away.

There was something standing in the corner. Or, rather, it was standing in the far corner of the living room's reflection—the reflection in the sliding glass door.

That would put it right next to me!

I looked over at the corner of the room, figuring this was it. It was the end for sure.

There was nothing there!

I turned my head back to the figure standing in the glass. Lightning bolts of fear traveled up and down my body, tickling my ribs with ice and making my hair stand on end.

I felt like one of those cartoons, stretched up high and eyes popping out with fright. Isn't this how it happened in the movies?

Good GOD! I'M in a MONSTER MOVIE! I thought. This wasn't good.

Through my fear, I studied this thing as I watched it glare at me. From my point of view, pressed back against the wall next to the record player, I could clearly see it in the lamp's light.

There was no mistaking it.

It was the Blood Banshee.

It wore an immaculate sheet like a cloak. Pointed nails at the end of its' feet poked from underneath the hem. Its hooded face came into the light as it approached me. Side two started to play.

The volume dial turned, by itself, all the way up. The first sounds, as you'd know if you've heard it, are a repeat of the Banshee's howl.

The noise hit the room like a freight train. I looked into its greedy yellow eyes.

The blue scales on its rubbery face parted ever wider, revealing its tusked mouth, big as a walrus. And the hand came up. A claw of matching blue scales reached out. Nails dug upward the same way it's pictured in the ad; pleading. It was calling out for my blood.

It took two shuffling steps towards me. My panic rose as I pressed myself back into the wall, and I felt my own howl rising. I was gonna scream! Scream like a little girl.

Then it turned and walked slowly across the reflection of the room, towards the edge of the door.

It didn't move like in the movies. It didn't ratchet or flick around super-fast. It just walked slowly, step by step, as if it knew that I couldn't do a thing about it.

It reached the side of the reflection and passed from view just as the howling on the record ceased. A very lame attempt at a werewolf call was next, but I wasn't even interested.

I looked into the darkness of the screen door. I was positive nothing was out there. I could see the bird feeder and the bushes at the back of the yard. It hadn't walked past the door.

By the time the ludicrous cries of a torture victim warbled on the record, I had worked up the courage to go to the door and slide it shut. I had to make sure it didn't come in from outside.

What was I thinking? How much more inside could it get? I couldn't think straight. I knew I had to close the door. I had to complete the reflection. I had to see where it had gone, even if it was gonna get me.

I could imagine sliding the door shut, and its reflection would be right there in my face. Or worse, the reflection of him standing behind me.

The sounds of a creeper moaning and pinching a screaming woman played in the background. He cackled in delight.

I put a hand on the door. I slid the door shut. I was, once again, all alone in the room.

I hadn't seen him as he'd moved through the reflection of the kitchen window or of any of the rooms along the first floor. All I knew was that he had gone. I didn't realize at the time where he had moved on to.

I didn't hear the screams of the neighbors three doors away and across the street. By all reports later, nobody had.

At some time that night, a whole family disappeared without a trace.

It took two weeks for someone to notice. Another week for the story to come out. That was long enough for me to fail to make the connection.

As it happened, both parents didn't show up for work, and their daughter didn't make it to school. Phone calls were made.

When all attempts at contact went unanswered, finally, the authorities were notified.

They entered a house that was as empty as the deck of a ghost ship. Beds were used. Their cars were in the driveway.

They were gone just like that.

Afterward, nobody knew how much further it went on. It was too widespread. The news agencies could have added things up had there been any reports.

It became a silent epidemic as years went by. Word of any incidents went unspoken. It wasn't even an urban legend.

How many thousands, thousands of families, fell victim to the alien visitor.

It took twenty-five years or more before it was brought to my attention. What had I unleashed on the world that night? What would it take to combat it?

The ad for the Gayle House Haunting sunk back into obscurity. The album was forgotten.

The killings went on, unknown to anyone, for decades.

Part One
Missing Persons

June 1993
Norwich, Connecticut 104 Main Street
the Mackenzies:
Family of Four

The Blood Banshee was on the loose.

It made its way through two other houses before it found its first victims. Passing behind the reflective surfaces saved so much time. It was his shuffling gait that left much to be desired.

It wasn't a fast creature by nature. It was slow at best, relying on its unnatural environment and shock tactics to confuse its prey.

And fear, oh, the delicious FEAR! Victims would be frozen to the spot, unable to even fight back as it tore them limb from limb in its powerful claws.

Fear added flavor to the kill. It spiced their blood like carbonated soda or fermented alcohol, only a thousandfold.

In these moments, his supernatural senses became enflamed. Glowing colors of spectral delight permeated the air around his human fodder. It flooded from their pores to light up the darkness.

It was actually for tracking his prey, but being immersed in it sent him into a killing frenzy.

Times like these might nourish him, but his chosen sustenance was the blood of little children. It was chosen, not by him but by the Creator. That was the decree. It was how he was made.

At the great beginning, the Creator had seen fit to invent him to punish the wicked. From prehistoric times it stalked the dark. It's what his kind was made for.

Everything, from the sluggish pace to the paralyzing venom in his four-inch extendable claws, was by design. Then there was the mode of travel.

Hidden in tiny spaces or moving from one shadow to another, he and his kind were the embodiment of the humans' worst nightmares.

Traveling through a reflected world, that was the Blood Banshee's special gift. The freedom of stalking behind the backdrop of any location at will, quasi-invisibility, and the invulnerability of a ghost was his to exploit.

He was a supernatural killing machine from the dawn of time.

Curse the devil that trapped him that made him subject to the playing of that infernal record disc.

That was the means of summoning him. It compelled him to come forth from the outer dimensions into mankind's existence. A foil to his natural stalking tactics, that what it was. Worse, he felt disjointed, held beyond his true form. It filled him with rage. He took his rage out on his victims. Only at times like these could he tear out a moment of peace, or such, that he could comprehend.

He had reached his destination. The home of a young couple with two infant children closed around him. The dresser mirror hung inverted before him.

He stood in a copy of the room down to the last detail. The young couple slept peacefully in their expensive beds. In the bed's doppelganger behind him: nothing. It was like that most of the time until he touched his victims. The fiend was not one interested in 'how' or 'why.' It needed only this.

Without preamble, it crawled through the opening created by the mirror frame. It slid over the dresser. It oozed across the floor.

His presence disturbed the young dreamers on a subconscious level. They twitched as their prosaic dreams soured into nightmares.

That was common, also. He invariably caused discomfort in his sleeping targets.

The beast did not even hesitate. It reached across the bed, wrapped the throat of the man and the woman in each paw, clutching them fiercely, and dragged them swiftly back through the breach in the wall.

This was the only element of discretion the killer had a presence of mind to maintain. It was all that was needed to ensure no one suspected: drag them, awake and mindless with horror, out of the direct line of sight. Beyond the edges of the mirror, he can butcher them with impunity.

No sound will reach back through the mirror. He can paint the very walls of this house-in-reverse with their fresh blood, leave their limbs and gutted bodies strewn down the hall. Not one trace of his passing will be visible.

The husband and wife disappeared from that world completely. He would have his fun.

The beast rode the killing frenzy. As it shredded the screaming couple before one another's streaming eyes, he bathed in their lifeblood.

Taking out his torment too quickly on the hapless humans left him more frustrated—this time. He had plans to make it better. No more, for him, the lure of the record. The accursed call, only to return after the player was destroyed, was not his way anymore. He had learned.

What the demon had in his insidious mind had to wait for now. He peered over his hunched shoulder at the children's room. There was a mirror mounted on the back of that closed door. He appeared within its depths and stared across the room at the frightened child.

A little girl.

The nightmares of her dismembered parents had awoken her. The Blood Banshee's unnatural glow, which happened only in front of frightened little children, began to illuminate the room.

She had a full view of his hunched form draped in white. His bright blue skin was covered in scales. Yellow eyes bored into her with an unblinking gaze. Under flaring nostrils gaped a leathery orifice lined with six-inch fangs.

The Fear rose off her quivering body in plumes. Crazy yellows, violent greens, and curdled violet streamed like northern lights up and up; until it billowed across the ceiling.

Her bladder let go, and the fumes of that aroma reached his nostrils. It enriched the savory effects. Saliva ran from his fanged maw in flood.

She began to scream.

"Mommy, Mommy! MOMMY!!!" reaching higher and higher in pitch.

A baby, the three-year old's younger brother, awoke, squalling from his crib in the corner. The dangling toys of the musical display hanging above him started to spin crazily. Eerie, disjointed music wheeled madly from its music box.

The Banshee could take no more. He let out his call, roaring in agonized rapture. In one step, he snatched up the boy-child and stuffed him in his mouth, swallowing him whole.

With one child silenced, the other increased her efforts. A fringe of lunacy was added to her cries. She was rooted to the spot, her sodden bedclothes reeking.

Yanking the corners of the little girl's bedsheets from the mattress, the monster took her up in a bundle, pausing to sample closer the fragrance of his piss-soaked catch.

He would drink deeply from this one. Deeply and slowly, once she was dragged across into his backward nether realm.

He will bite off her head, swallowing it like he did her baby brother. Holding his mouth over her spouting neck veins, he will guzzle the arterial flow straight down his throat. Then suck greedily until, only by squeezing her frail body and wringing her like a dishrag, would he be sure to get every last drop. The crunch and squish of bone and flesh were, ever, so sublime.

Slugging the struggling bundle over one shoulder, he stepped unhurriedly through the mirror on the door.

After waiting in limbo for twenty-five years, this had been a perfect beginning. Now, secure in anonymity, he would take his sustenance.

The drool left in the children's shag carpet will have dried clear long before any inspectors arrived. The girl's missing sheets will only add to the mystery.

It was two weeks before Missing Persons sent anyone to investigate.

August 1993
Providence, Rhode Island
Memorial Hospital

"Really, Mrs. Reilly. You should have us take a closer look."

The nurse was being persistent for a good reason. The child was brought in with a broken arm. It was the other bruises that caught her attention. She knew layers when she saw them. A clumsy attempt to strike the little girl only in the same places would look like that.

From the thick layer of makeup her disheveled mother wore, she could guess what shades of color would lay underneath: dirty yellows, smoky violet, faded black.

"No, no, no…" The tired-looking woman said a little too quickly. "We have to be home. It's time for me to start supper and Delilah still has chores."

She couldn't register the nurse's raised eyebrow at that last part with her eyes cast towards the ground. She fumbled with her daughter's good hand in distraction.

The nurse was still taken aback. She really shouldn't be surprised. She was appalled though she had expected it. Mrs. Reilly may have been a good woman, at one time, before she was married.

She hadn't once hugged her daughter or tried to comfort her at all today. She only gave some lame excuse for the state of the stairs. Poor Delilah had been playing on, even chastised the doomed little girl.

The only reason she was holding her hand now was in case someone tried to take her. They could make a run for it—what a world.

It was almost time for Nurse Chapman to be finishing her shift and thinking about dinner herself. With a sigh, she made up her mind.

"If you could just wait here a moment, I'll have the doctor sign a slip excusing Delilah from school." She couldn't get out of that examination room fast enough.

The nurse closed the door as gently as she could. "Probably headed to the phone right now." The mother said to herself.

"Your Paw sure won't take kindly to any interference," she said down to the girl.

Delilah only sat with her head down, the fresh new cast clutched on her dingy lap. Her feet dangled listlessly above the floor.

The battered wife crossed the examination room to the mirror. Leaning over to inspect her makeup (this ain't foolin' no one), she spoke over her shoulder at her daughter.

"If he catches wind of anything out of sorts…"

The little girl noticed a moment went by without her mother lecturing her. She could have sworn she had more to say. Delilah looked up from under her dirty hair. Where had her mother gone?

Was she behind the screen? No. The sunlight through the window would have shown up her shadow on it from behind.

"Momma?" she ventured on instinct.

She got up off the chair timidly. Sure of a beating, she too crossed the exam room. The last place her mother was standing was here by the sink. There was a small step stool in front of it she hadn't thought to use before. Water must be preserved. Her Dadda always said.

There was a pounding noise, muffled, coming from right in front of her. She stepped up on the step stool and looked in the mirror. Wasn't it a mirror?

There was Momma. She was standing in the next room pounding on the window. She looked scared. She kept looking behind her, then hammering her fists against the glass more feverishly.

Suddenly, her arm shot straight out to her side. She pulled and pulled, but her arm wouldn't budge.

"Let go, let go!!!" she yelled at absolutely nothing. Her cries could barely be heard. Then, with a sickening 'SNAP!' the lower half of her forearm bent completely out of place. It was as if someone invisible had just snapped her arm in two!

Delilah was hammering her tiny fists on her side of the glass now, too. She yelled for her momma as she faded from view. All she was left with was her own reflection.

And the great, big thing standing behind her!

She looked into the bugged-out eyes of a blue-faced monster standing over her reflection. He wore a white sheet like it was a hood or a robe. Fangs like tusks dripped all over her. She could feel it now. She could feel his breath panting on her neck.

It reached down to her reflection's shoulders with scaly blue paws from behind, and she felt those paws placed on her.

In that instant, she found she was on the other side of the glass looking at herself in the examination room they had come in. Her mother was a crumpled heap on the floor. She cradled her broken arm, rocking in madness at the girl's feet.

Delilah's last sight, as she turned to look up behind her, was of the Blood Banshee as it opened its mouth so wide. It sank its fangs through her neck, and the image of herself in the window faded from the room.

When Nurse Chapman returned, she was followed by the doctor and two orderlies in case it was necessary to restrain the mother and separate the girl. She had called Child Services and the police. Both were on the way.

It looked like she would have to apologize to them when they arrived. Mrs. Reilly and her daughter were gone.

"That's the third time this month." an orderly complained. "They just took off."

Nurse Chapman wasn't going to be outrun. She gave Child Services the Reillys' address. They showed up the next day to find an irate Mr. Reilly without his wife and daughter to wait on him. He raged about how his wife had taken his daughter and left him.

This was one of several disappearances that were not attributed to the Rhode Island Hospital though they actually happened on its floors.

Within its walls, five other children had been finished with their appointments and, along with their parents, failed to leave. Hospital staff only assumed they had.

One extreme incident caused enough uproar to even make the papers but the Night Nurse in the newborn nursery and the nine babies she had, reportedly, stolen were never found. It was suspected she had an accomplice because her car was left in her parking spot.

September 1995
Rochester, New York
Rustic Village Apartments

Like an infestation of bed bugs, the apartment complex was besieged though no one would ever know of it. As close together as they live, it was not like everyone knew each other. Neighbors might share ten square feet of doorstep at the top of a cement stairwell, but doormats were all they would see of one another.

Two hundred and eight families shared the eighty thousand square foot parcel where the first phase of buildings were laid down. By 1995, sixteen complexes became two hundred.

Seven thousand families and growing, by the turn of the Millennium, came and went. The management had its share of walkouts, or so they thought. Whole families leaving without notice happened more often than not.

Combined with the regular complaints by tenants of 'less than natural' activity, it was not a surprise if apartments were abandoned in the night filled with all their belongings.

More mysterious were the sudden departures without notice, especially without any sign of a moving van. The apartment would be cleaned out of all belongings. Not a piece of furniture was left. No witnesses could claim to know just when their neighbors had left. One night, the apartment next door would go silent.

It was like the domiciles had never been occupied aside from the official records. You would think someone might stop at the manager's office to, at least, argue over the security deposit.

Strange and disquieting, it had prompted the management, after confirming their sanity, to stop asking questions of the remaining families and to organize a very effective cover-up.

They became unwitting accomplices to the Blood Banshee's clandestine rampage. They thought it was just a run of the mill haunting.

Everyone saw Poltergeist on HBO. Did anyone really get hurt? It was just a few families skipping out on their last rent. Such lowlifes were unwelcome.

Better to not let it get around that the place was haunted or that families were disappearing. That would hurt business, with flats coming open all the time. They couldn't afford anyone being scared off before they moved in.

October 1997
Pittsburgh, Pennsylvania

The Blood Banshee circled its way around the New England countryside. Moving through broad daylight, he joined the reflections of the pedestrians as they crowded the city sidewalks.

The human cattle were so engrossed with their daily lives they never looked deep enough into the mirrored glare of the storefronts to see the grotesque creature, wrapped in white, staring murderous intent from across a street.

Once in a while, someone, invariably a child, would catch a glimpse of him and single themselves out for the killer to follow home.

Little Susan Bradford was shopping for a Halloween costume. She was ten years old and fully capable of walking the three blocks down to Lincoln Avenue. The corner drug store had costumes and masks and makeup.

There were many people walking on the sidewalk and a constant flow of traffic in the street. Cars rushed by, trying to beat the traffic lights.

Uncarved pumpkins and stalks of corn husks adorned the stoops of every shop. There were store-bought decorations in the windows. Suzie loved Halloween, and it was still a few weeks away, so she started the season window shopping.

Peering into the dress maker's store, she thought she saw a bedsheet ghost being reflected back at her from across the street. Squinting her eyes into focus, she could swear the thing was looking straight at her. It faced her, all right. She could just make out that its face was blue.

She turned to see the neat Halloween decoration across the street, but it wasn't there.

Turning back to the glass, she could faintly see the wedding dress deep in the little shop through the glare on the window. Is that what she saw?

She moved on down the street. Beyond the edge of her vision, the creature in white kept pace.

The girl turned her head to look at the decorations in an old bookshop, and the stalker froze in place. She could plainly see it hunched over the edge of the sidewalk staring at her.

She turned violently to look at it and almost tripped over her own feet.

Righting herself to look directly across the street, she saw that, once again, her eyes had deceived her. There was a bedsheet in front of the barbershop hanging up to look like a ghost.

She turned to the window, again, to look at its reflection, to confirm it was what she thought she saw. The Blood Banshee was there standing plainly in front of the barber's pole. It stood in front of the bedsheet ghost!

People walked to and fro. Cars filed by in both directions, and this thing was focused entirely on her.

She couldn't move. She stared at the reflection in horror. The thing took a step forward, off the curb. She almost backed into the street.

She bumped into a lady walking by. The woman said, "excuse me," peevishly. When Suzie looked back at the reflection, she expected the creature would be gone. It was not.

As a matter of fact, it had not stopped walking forward. It moved right into traffic. The speeding cars never slackened their pace. The drivers did not register its presence.

Suzie looked from side to side in a panic. Did anyone else walking around her see this?

She spun to face the street. It wasn't there!

She faced the window again. It was right on top of her.

She stood reflected at herself, and this blue-faced thing rose up from the street right behind her! It reached out a scaly blue claw at her back as she aimed herself towards home and bolted.

She ran full speed for two blocks, dodging and weaving through the complaining foot traffic, before holing up in a doorway to catch her breath.

She peeked around the corner. It wasn't following her on the sidewalk. She continued home, passing the last of the shops. One by one, her reflection kept pace with her.

From her angle, she was unable to see the beast that scuttled just behind her reflection, following it home.

When she was past the shops and had turned down Hawley, she thought she was safe. Nobody was in a position to see that a monster was abroad in full daylight, invisible to the naked eye.

Passing through the mirror image on the front door and window of each house, the reflection of little Suzie Bradford was bringing the Blood Banshee home for supper.

The monster settled in at the center of the house. He was prepared to spend days tormenting the Bradford family. The fiend had been perfecting his art.

It began small. Car keys were moved from the last place they were left. By the third time, replacing the keys back in their original spot only after the search was carried out, he moved on to bigger scares.

Mr. Bradford became suspicious of his daughter. She must have been playing pranks. No matter how fiercely she denied it, his anger only rose higher.

They yelled in each other's faces until Mrs. Bradford hollered at them both.

At the table, too much salt found its way into Mr. Bradford's dinner. Suzie was automatically the culprit. Nobody ate as the volume of their tempers increased.

Suzie was scolded by her mother and sentenced to wash the dishes as punishment. She made the attempt.

One by one, plates smashed on the floor before her horror-struck eyes.

Her father had finally reached the end of his patience, sending her to bed with no tv.

The Blood Banshee pulled out all the stops. Objects began to hurl themselves at Mr. Bradford. Heavy objects. A decorative marble ashtray. His nine iron from his set of golf clubs. Mr. and Mrs. Bradford were now terrified beyond all reason.

The Blood Banshee decided now was the time to strike. The girl had come to the bedroom door to find out what was wrong with daddy. Her parents were making their way to her room.

Suzie stood in her doorway, anticipating their accusations. Just as she realized they were starting to apologize, she was yanked into the room by an invisible force. Her door slammed shut in the couple's faces.

They pounded on the door and tried turning the knob. Mr. Bradford began ramming a shoulder into it. Nothing worked, and the squealing cries of their little girl reached higher and higher pitches.

Suddenly, she stopped. All was quiet except the hinges on Suzie's door as it softly swung open.

Mr. and Mrs. Bradford were unprepared to discover her room was empty, but there it was. There was no sign of her.

The window was shut, and her closet was open. Looking under the bed (nothing there), they swung up to find the mirror on her dresser had more in it than just the reflection of Suzie's empty room.

Their little Suzie was pinned to the wall. Her head hung down lifelessly.

They made the mistake of leaning forward for a closer look.

Their parting view in this lifetime was the gaping jaws and jutting fangs of the yellow-eyed demon whose blue face popped up in the mirror. With a blood-curdling howl, it reached forward with its scaly blue claws and snatched them by the tops of their heads. It dragged them headfirst into the open mirror, kicking and screaming.

The image reflected in the mirror returned to the view of an empty room. The sounds of the Bradfords being dismembered were trapped behind the glass.

The Blood Banshee occupied himself with the Bradfords for the weeks and months it took to rent the house out to another family. He enacted all the same terrors on them, too, as well as the two families that followed.

When he was through with those, the house stood empty. Word had got out of the strange disappearances and the soft screaming. Sometimes they were heard after the house was known to be empty. It gained a reputation in Pittsburgh.

When paranormal investigators arrived, they were disappointed to experience nothing.

The Blood Banshee was long gone.

Part Two
Claura's Tale

Beccaria, Pennsylvania
139 Elizabeth Street
October 2007

1. Arrival

Claura Roberts had not grown up on Elizabeth Street. If she'd had a choice, she would never have moved there. Didn't the girls in school understand that? She didn't want her there any more than they did.

The kids in school had lived their whole lives in that dead-end valley.

Set in the left armpit of Pennsylvania, Beccaria was the furthest point from anything. All it took was putting a street of houses deep in the center of a square bordered by highways. Then put all the businesses, all the stores, all the restaurants, right off the highway.

You used a tank of gas to drive all the way to the station to fill up so you could get home. That wasn't the running joke. It was a statement of fact.

Elizabeth Street wound through the wood line like a varicose vein in an octogenarian's leg. It couldn't have been a quarter-mile between the 254 and the old paper mill. Two miles of houses were wrapped up in that silly string of an excuse for a road.

Every six months, a crew would come through and "salt the gravel," sealing it with fresh oil. The grass to either side went untended. Trees fell where they may.

The houses jutted from the mossy green gumline of the nearest mountain ridges like a hobo's grimace.

Fully nine out of every ten homes were uninhabitable. They were just left there to rot like old barns and sheds you see from the freeway. Weeds and brush were all that resided there, now, and they asserted themselves up to the caved-in rooftops.

Each window was afflicted with the broken glass disease, and some showed off their collapsed flooring through their missing front doors.

Claura couldn't help thinking how the children were representative of the same entropy. Their humor was primitive. Their grunted comments were neanderthal. Claura didn't know girls could grunt.

They practically thumped their saggy chests territorially, turning zit-effaced noses up at her presence.

She just smiled back in disdain. She knew they were jealous. After all, it took several generations of them to produce a full set of teeth.

They hated her because she was too pretty. In the last school system, they hated her because she was too white.

On top of everything else, there was nothing to do here. The nearest Walmart was thirty miles, as the crow flies. Fifty-eight miles by road.

Rollercoasters had fewer twists and turns. They didn't have the added luxury of hot and cold running deer or drunk drivers to force you off the road. You didn't have to pay to get that sort of entertainment but, if you weren't lucky, you'd wind up paying for it, nonetheless.

139 was a blue, two-story house that her mother rented from a friend of hers. It was in her family from back when they had settled in the area.

Her friend lived in Ohio.

It used fuel oil for heat in the winter and an open door to cool it off on summer nights. There was no back door.

To go for a walk, there was only a block of streets running down the hill before the front door. It only amounted to ten thousand square feet before coming around to the door again.

An abandoned brick store with enormous plate glass windows adorned the opposite side of the street, which descended across from the token porch.

Of the surrounding houses, only two weren't total habitats. One sat on the other side of the street. It faced the run down artifacts from behind the shield of an oak, which stood directly in the way of its front door.

Most of the limbs had been trimmed under low hanging electrical wires. The remainder arched back over the second story, gripping the roof of the house possessively. The building itself was a dwarf, barely more than ten feet deep.

It stood, locked in its strangeness. Claura couldn't tell if anyone really lived there.

The only other house on that end of Elizabeth sporting inhabitants sat high on its hill at the end of the street. Its paint was fresh like the planters on the porch. Wind chimes sang softly in its eaves.

The family that lived there were older but lively. They were visible and seemed to enjoy the outside of their house just as much as being within it.

They had set plastic lawn chairs in the back yard, perhaps, by a fire pit. It was hard to see what was up there from the road. They held court early in the evening as if watching the back of the house were a spectator sport.

They had moved in a few months after Claura, and her mother had arrived, and it did not look like they came from around there, even from a distance.

Their voices carried easily from down the street. Their accents were clean with no hint of a twang, northern or southern. They could be seen enjoying a glass of wine.

Just their presence was a sign of life that set their yard apart from the rest of the street. Beneath their oaks was a glimpse back into civilization.

Claura could tell her mother felt comforted in knowing they were there though she never acknowledged it.

They had never met.

That's all there was to the neighborhood. The forest was packed thick with brush and nearly vertical up the side of the mountain, so no going for a walk in these woods.

There wasn't any money to spare even if there were someplace to spend it. If it weren't for the Internet, Claura would have lost her mind. At least there was cable service for the TV. The town only got two local channels. Thank God for Netflix.

Her mother would only watch Buffy the Vampire Slayer or Supernatural. At least she liked SOME monsters.

All things creepy, that was Claura's passion.

She didn't consider herself gothic or emo. She just knew what was cool.

She'd eased up on the mascara just recently. Her mother was quite relieved. She still dyed her hair blue. All her clothes had holes in their knees. They started to sell them like that now, anyway.

Searching the Internet for haunted houses and paranormal accounts whiled away the time. Real-life accounts of serial killers had begun showing up alongside fan fiction and dark poetry.

The more elaborate sites shared work that just could not be substantiated. She enjoyed the nightmarish fantasy of a slasher film come to life. The variety was beginning to rival the shock and gore of the big screen.

She knew none of it was true. Urban legends were just that. Legends. Legends were made up by people. Greek mythology couldn't be based on fact. It's an endless supply of monsters made for good stop motion animated fun, though.

She wasn't a big fan of those kinds of monsters. Godzilla and Gamera were kid stuff. Frankenstein and Dracula were for geeks and toy collectors.

Anyone that said they believed in vampires was just dressing up and needed to get a life and lay off the Twilight novels. Like Harry Potter, it's fun to dress up as your favorite character, but everyone knows that kind of magic doesn't exist.

You dress up once a year at Halloween. On any other day, it's just creepy in a thirty-eight-year-old-living-in-mommy and daddy's-basement creepy kind of way.

He's fat as hell, but, boy, does he have a killer toy collection. No job to speak of but spends all his allowance on comic books.

Dating was the furthest thing from Claura's mind, and it was a good thing, too. Boys only thought about getting a girl that would put out. They would never consider they weren't attractive. That wasn't part of the equation for boys who had beards to finish out their duck hunter fashion. Yuck.

What made them think a girl was just automatically attracted to them just because he noticed you were there and you had a pulse. Pulse optional for these creeps, for sure.

Claura wondered how many of their dates met with a "hunting accident" if they didn't give it up.

They were, obviously, willing to look past her grim wardrobe. She could see the look in their eyes as they imagined what was underneath it. But she doesn't put out, so they quickly lost interest.

Thank God. she could do without the teasing, though. If you're not a whore, then you must be a prude, right?

That wasn't half as bad as the way the girls treated her. They glared at her. They played dirty pranks on her. Who wants to go to a place every day where you're told to your face that you're not welcome?

Claura had received her share of abuse in different school systems since she was a child. She had always been friendly and knew how to be a good friend.

After leaving a string of friends in so many places, she lost count. The level of bile she faced now, at the age of 17, was going to get to her.

"You live on Elizabeth Street?!" They asked her in mocked sympathy. "That's where poor families go to disappear. Everyone knows the Boogeyman lives there. He goes from house to house like the tooth fairy."

"One day, you'll wake up disappeared, too!" A real bunch of closet intellectuals here.

It was almost enough to make someone as forgiving as her wish someone would make them pay. Their wicked behavior was mindless. It would take somebody even more mindless to put them in their place.

Six feet under, Claura allowed herself to think, but only jokingly.

Only joking.

Lately, Claura couldn't help feeling like she had drawn the attention of something with her torment. Something that understood how she felt.

Once, she had gone for a walk around the block. There was no one around. Five houses comprised the residences (actively inhabited) down the street and around the corner.

It wasn't like the wind sighing over the mountain called her by name or anything.

What she did hear was a distant roaring. It sounded as if a giant beast was trapped somewhere on the other side of the ridgeline. It poured over the top, bringing with it a gust of wind rushing at her like an avalanche. It tossed her hair and grabbed at her whole being, almost knocking her from her feet.

Convinced the blowing wind was the source of the groaning call, she ducked around the next corner and came past the old brick store.

The red brick seemed brighter today—some trick of the light. The sky was gloomy. Dark clouds rushed over the horizon. Sunlight from the opposite direction highlighted everything.

The wind pushed past her like an impatient pedestrian. Claura clutched herself with both arms, hunching forward and quickening her pace.

She passed the storefront windows. There was a time when people would come from the sawmill down the street and meet at the diner's counter. They would discuss things of that time. Now only the empty room looked back out at her from behind the tall glass, waiting beneath its layer of dust.

Just then, Claura received a text message. It was from her mother telling her to be home for dinner. Where else was she supposed to go? She stood beside the window, looking down at her phone.

She didn't glimpse the lonely figure stepping from the wood line across the street.

It stood without moving. She didn't see it because it only appeared in the glass. She would have seen it if it were truly across the road.

The Blood Banshee was drawn to this girl by her anguish. She would present him with something he knew—a fresh situation, perhaps.

Perhaps he would be performing his true function after all this time. The Blood Banshee could taste righteous fury and vindication on this one.

Claura looked up, focusing on the way she was headed. Walking neck and neck with her reflection, she didn't see the shuffling creature that fell into step behind it.

As she reached the edge of the yard, two feet of overgrown grass to either side of a patch of gravel, her rat terrier/chihuahua mix dog named Junior could be heard barking his little head off.

He barked at everything. Often he seemed to bark at nothing, standing on the back of the couch to force his way through the curtains of the front bay window—cars, people at their houses hundreds of feet away, a blowing leaf.

It was infuriating to have him barking at you when you came home. He knew who it was. They lived there! But he would still bark and bark till you were three feet in the door, yelling at him, "GO TO BED!"

Hardly willing to relent, he would go to the dog bed behind the lamp table. A final "woof" still escaping him as he reluctantly squatted on his pillow.

This day, after Claura's latest walk, Junior began to bark, as usual. As Claura stepped in the door, Junior was still barking.

As she drew in a breath to scold the over-eager guardian, Junior's gaze swung to the space directly behind her.

The dog froze in place. His ears slumped back. His tail shot between his legs. He even pee-ed a little, but he scrambled to his corner, suddenly afraid to make any sound.

He didn't come out until Claura had gone to bed.

Claura had to do the dishes from the day before so there would be room to cook.

Dinner was non-descript. They couldn't afford much food stamps. If they had taken something out of the freezer to thaw, they wouldn't have had to resort to grilled cheese sandwiches. She seemed to be eating a lot of them lately.

Her mother wasn't feeling well again. She couldn't blame her for having such bad health. It was just the way things were. She learned long ago how to roll with the punches. She just wanted to be a good daughter and not add to the strain on her mother.

So, with supper out of the way, Claura could move on with the rest of her evening.

Sunday night meant there was school tomorrow. She needed to take a shower and wash her hair. Right now, she could see what was on the Internet.

"Claura! It's time for your shower, honey." her mother called from downstairs. She had lost track of time. This happens when you don't have an alarm clock. Or a nightstand.

She stayed in the room upstairs that wasn't filled with old junk. The darkroom where she slept was so small there wouldn't have been room for furniture if they presently had any. It was a wonder any space had been found for a window. It was covered by a curtain as its reward. Very nondecorative. The whole house had the look of a storage unit.

The only sign of habitation was her unmade bed and piles of worn clothes on the floor. It reinforced the notion that this place was only temporary. At this point, it had become intentional.

After her shower, she stood before the mirror at the bathroom sink. It was the only mirror in the whole house. As she raised her hand to wipe the steamed surface clear, she thought she saw something.

Theoretically, she supposed she had. It was impossible to see much of her reflection in that surface, but what she could make out was wider than her, and the halo she expected of her soaked, blue hair was not her silhouette but looked as if the whole face were blue.

That was the impression she got from behind the condensation on the mirrored glass.

She held the white towel around herself with one hand. The other swiped across, wiping away the fog. Her fresh face with bedraggled, wet hair inspected her right back.

She didn't think any further about it.

That night, she had the first nightmare she could remember having since she was a little girl. All she could see in the dream were a glowing pair of yellow eyes.

She woke up the next morning with a pounding headache that the sunlight only made worse. Better than that, she had a scratch around one forearm that was impossibly deep.

Her nails weren't sharp enough to cause such a long gash. She would have to wear long sleeves today.

2. Encounters

Another miserable day of school made an attempt to materialize. Claura could not identify the problem. Something was bugging her, and she didn't understand why.

She was surrounded by the strangers she had been riding the bus with since the end of last school year. Why did she have a feeling like she was being watched?

Nobody paid any attention to her, as usual.

And, from time to time, she caught something from the corner of her eye. Oddly, it seemed to be a reflection in the bus window across the aisle. Nobody was sitting in the seat.

Every time she turned to look out the window, only the dark Pennsylvania forest rushed by. Facing forward, she could almost see it again.

It was a white blur as if something hung right outside, lit by the glare of the internal lighting. It moved alongside the window, never wavering, and bounced along with the movement of the bus.

Again, she looked, and it was gone. It had begun to get light out with the coming of dawn, and all things dark would be banished, once again, until nightfall—another day just like any other.

Nothing would be further from the truth.

All during her first class, Claura had trouble concentrating. And in her second class, it got even worse.

A rushing noise seemed to fill her ears, accompanied by an increased pressure in her head. Maybe she was coming down with something.

By the third class, she felt a twinge of nausea that had her raising her hand to go to the restroom.

She felt like she wasn't walking the hallway alone. The whole way there, she kept looking over her shoulder at the empty halls behind her. Every step felt like someone wasn't just following her but walking at her shoulder. Every few feet was a classroom door and, at even intervals, a mirror.

She was seeing it out of the corner of her eye again. A great white blur like laundry waving on a clothesline. Clearly, there was something stalking right next to her. She could feel, again, that breath on her neck. It just wouldn't let her see it.

Faster and faster she went. When the panting beside her became loud enough to cover the sound of her own panicked breathes, she started to run.

At the intersection of the halls, she tried to run full tilt to the left. An errant gust of wind roared in her face.

She spun around to go right instead. Leaving the growl building in the air behind, she felt like she was being herded to the restroom at the far end of the school complex.

Hitting the bathroom door at top speed, she slammed through the door and almost into-for the love of everything holy—the three people she least wanted to see. Like, ever.

Becky Turner and her two sidekicks looked up from the cigarette they were shared by the open window. By the malicious smiles emerging from their faces, Claura could tell she must have just made their day.

"Well, well, well," said Becky, flipping her blonde hair from her pimpled brow. "Looky here, girls. If it isn't the homecoming float right into our hate parade."

Shawnee Bryce didn't know what her bossy friend was trying to say, really, but the intent was clear. Shawnee was a very pretty girl. For that reason, Becky preferred to dominate her. She had since childhood and, as a result, had held back Shawnee's intellectual development to be a respectful step behind her's at all times.

Roberta 'Big Berta' Jonesboro never spoke much. She was just along for the malevolence. It took only a haughty snort or guffaw to convey her brutish thoughts. After all, Becky did all the talking.

"Now's not a good time, you guys," Claura warned. " I think you better get out of here."

"Listen ta THAT!" Shawnee barked in surprise. "Who does she think she's talking to?"

"Ho-hoooh!" Bertha chortled.

"Really?!" Becky was practically shouting, "You come to our town. You burst into our territory? I've just been waiting for you to give me a reason to mess up that pretty face."

She had backed Claura up against the sinks. Bending her backward by the benefit of getting in her face, she made to reach up and make good on her threat.

The Blood Banshee had had his fill of anguish. Wicked children! This was the torment that dragged him here, forced him towards this moment. He was helpless in this one respect, and the torrent of emotion drove him over the edge.

With one step, he was through the reflection of Claura's back. Facing her tormentor, the beast rose from over Claura's shoulder and stared right into Becky Turner's bugged-out eyes with yellow ones of his own.

The other two bullies couldn't see. Claura's back was to it. Only Becky could see it.

Before Becky had time to scream, the Blood Banshee reached out and grabbed her by the hair.

To Shawnee and Berta, it looked like the two girls were having a hair-pulling contest. When it appeared that their friend was losing, they jumped forward to lend a hand.

Without so much as sparing them a look, the Blood Banshee brought up a gust of wind and fury. It was an invisible hand that launched both girls back and through the stall doors of the toilets to crash in twin heaps. Both landings were equally painful. The creature had made his point.

Releasing the struggling child, for now, the would-be attacker flung herself backward. She busted into the toilet in between.

With a single burst of his mournful howl, the Blood Banshee disappeared from view. Claura, shivering in her bones, slowly turned. Her head jittered on a swivel.

Her fear was running high. Sputtering breathes heaved arrhythmically in her lungs. She stood quaking at the empty mirror. The only living thing visible was sprawled aching in the three toilet stalls.

"Remember," she obliged. "I tried to warn you." And walked out with as much calm as she could muster.

Things were never going to be the same.

3. Along For the Ride

The rest of the day passed. Claura was unable to register much of it. The nature of her lack of relationships served its purpose. She was able to get through the remainder of her classes and onto the school bus without anybody else bothering her, but she was in a daze.

She expected at any moment to sense that haunting feeling that started her day, but the sensation had fled.

She spent a peaceful evening at home. Junior barked his little head off as she'd stepped through the door. There were the dishes and dinner, homework and tv.

She even enjoyed a long shower, and nothing appeared in the mirror after. It seemed things were going normal.

She could have believed that if it wasn't for her dreams. While she tossed and turned in her sheets, she was stalking down the road. Everything was backward. She could tell.

She looked down at her feet. Toenails, as long as cutting knives, revealed themselves back and forth. It was a rhythm of determined footsteps. They poked out from under the bedsheet she was wearing.

She tried to lick her drooling lips only to be introduced to an array of enormous teeth. Claura could feel their length with her tongue, test their sharpness.

She looked up at the house she stood before. The name "Turner" was on the mailbox in reverse.

A wave of disorientation crashed over her. She found herself looking into a girl's bedroom from a small window above the dresser.

Becky had just sat down at her dressing table in her lavish bedroom. Pop music played loudly on her stereo. She thought she was going to brush her hair after taking her shower. It had taken extra-long for her to calm her nerves and soothe her aching back.

It never occurred to her that she could be in any danger. In a single moment, her complacency caught up with her. She looked past herself, deep in the mirror.

It stood there in the corner. That thing that attacked her in the school bathroom was staring at her back. From the top of its scaly blue skull and over the tips of its clawed toes hung a burial shroud that it wore like a hooded cloak. The burning yellow eyes bored into her once again.

Whatever the thing was, it had protected Claura. She hadn't been ready to release her anger over that. The indignation was more than she was willing to forget.

The Blood Banshee's appearance solved that real quick. She certainly wasn't thinking about her pride anymore. Not with that thing standing behind her.

Claura immediately saw the waves of color surging out of her rival. First came the look of shock. Next came the torrent of glowing light in every sickening shade of the spectrum and some not normally detected by the human eye.

It was a physical manifestation of Becky's fear. Pheromones, she thought they were called. It bothered her how excited they made her feel.

She tried to remember she was asleep. This couldn't be happening, but she had never felt more awake. The beast had her riding behind its eyes.

She couldn't move. Her body would not obey her commands. That's when she realized it was not her body. She could sense its thoughts. She could tell which ones weren't her own. She had a moment to delve into it. She pulled back in quickly in revulsion, but not without getting what sounded like a name.

Blood Banshee.

Becky's pheromone level shot up as the reflection scuttled right for her back.

With a hoarse intake of breath, Becky was up from her chair and whirled around in shock.

There was nobody there.

She gave up brushing her hair. Facing away from the mirror, she actually thought she was safe. She thought she might get a decent night's sleep, too.

Every time she turned out the light and tried to lay down, she could see the thing glowing in the corner. Drool was pouring onto its feet. It panted like a grizzly bear when she shut her eyes.

"Mom! Dad!" she cried. Calling for her parents received the predictable response. They even scolded her, the bullies that had raised her.

"Why don't you stop having nightmares and get some sleep!" they told her.

By Wednesday, she showed up at school looking like roadkill. Claura thought she would be more pleased. That was the beast talking.

Meanwhile, Shawnee was dumped on the floor beside her bed every night at exactly 2:30.

Claura was there. She witnessed the approach to her house, the wave of dizziness; then she was propelled into a bedroom to take part in tossing the sleeping girl from her mattress.

Once again, the colors of fear lit up the dark. Claura could feel them seething within her. It was delicious in a way she felt ashamed of. To watch the snotty little bitch sprawled on the floor, The comical way her head darted back and forth, trying to see an invisible intruder, was amusing. But this other feeling, like a bully teasing a defenseless animal, made her sick. And the cravings. What was THAT about?

Later, they were at the trailer home of Berta Bryce.

Berta felt a tremendous blow as if something were punching her in the gut. Twice she woke up struggling to breathe with the wind knocked out of her.

Claura saw this happening as if she, herself, were in the beast's place. Every night, the two of them, as one, went to each girl's house and did the same thing. She didn't know who was getting more worn out, her or them.

Every morning she awoke refreshed.

Berta showed up for school on Thursday with a black eye.

They were living in fear at school, too. Every reflective surface they could see him. Even ones he was not in.

They were being worn down.

"Are you guys seeing it too?" Becky asked her cohorts on Friday. "I thought you were both acting funny."

"Nuthin' funny about this." Big Berta rumbled. Shawnee just shivered and tried to hide her tears.

"Not one word of this!" Becky commanded. "Do you want to wind up in Torrance?" she hissed at them over the lunch table. "I'm not going to be put away because of that bitch!" The other two looked more reluctant to obey her than they were willing to admit to themselves.

In the end, they agreed. They couldn't tell anyone.

Claura was cornered again in the girl's locker room. This time the three bullies kept a respectful distance. Becky, as usual, took the lead.

"What's the big idea?!" She shouted.

"I have no clue what you're bragging about," Claura retorted. "But you look like shit."

"None of us have slept in days," Shawnee muttered. She kept glancing around like a cornered animal.

"What did you do to us?" Berta chimed in.

"I didn't do a damned thing," Claura replied, caustic wit returning. She found facing these three morons increasingly easy now.

"Try interrogating your own guilt. You might get some insight into how you've been treating people."

"You sicked that thing on us!" Becky was almost in tears. "Call it off or else."

Claura found herself rising to the challenge like never before. She stepped right up to Becky and pressed her nose to nose.

"Or else WHAT?!" The dangerous note in Claua's voice made the other girls flinch back, inadvertently.

They muttered sounds that didn't quite regain their bravado. In the end, the trio spun on their heels and headed for the door.

Claura was stunned. Where had that come from? She looked around. And what were they talking about? Her dreams?

She hadn't believed her experiences were anything like that. She watched them go. They were filing out the door like scolded puppies.

Passing one more mirror at the threshold, Becky turned, flanked by her reflection, and gave Claura a last accusatory glance.

Claura shook her head in wonder. What a fake show of strength. She kept her eyes on them as they left from sight. Then, just before the door closed behind them, she caught the clearest look at it.

It shuffled into sight across the mirror's confines. It headed for the door in the girls' wake. Claura was taken aback and filled with dread. Was she seeing this?

A big, blue scaly beast was stalking the other girls. It wore some kind of burial shroud-like. It was a cloak. Its clawed feet were enormous. It turned once as it reached the reflection of the door and fixed her in its deadly gaze.

Its yellow eyes struck her almost physically. They were set in the face of pure evil. Bright blue and craggy, its scaly cheekbones jutted out like rocky outcroppings of turquoise in a sea of menace. A stub of a nose floated, there, in between, nostrils flaring.

Lumpy edges of, what served as lips, surrounded a cluster of dripping fangs. They were each at least four inches long!

Drooling in anticipation, its mouth turned up in an approximation of a smile. It clearly enjoyed what it was doing. It held one gigantic claw to its lips, warning silence, then disappeared out the mirror's door. It was trying to be funny, but the threat was so real.

That night, Claura's thoughts on the bathroom mirror took on a whole new dimension. Perhaps she was safe because it was too small for the scaly assailant to fit through.

Staring into its depths for what she knew was far too long, she dared the thing to show itself. Tempting fate never feels wrong until it catches you, and catch her, it did.

Like a bear defending itself, the monster shot up into view. Claura didn't have time to scream as it reached for her with one massive paw. It had to turn and press its head against the inside of the wall to reach out at her.

What was she talking about? How could this be? Was it really stuck in the wall or transcending some ancient dimension in space and reality?

This thought was her last before being consumed by the searing pain.

The Blood Banshee had caught hold of her arm. Four clawed nails bit into her as it raked furrows in her flesh. A supernatural cold spread throughout her body, locking her in place. Claura was paralyzed by its venom. With a single foam-flecked roar, it plunged from sight.

Claura was still standing there three hours later when her mother returned from shopping.

"Are you cutting yourself, again?"

Her mother asked.

"Don't be crazy," Claura replied. "If I were, don't you think I'd be hiding it from you?"

"If it's those girls, we can report them to the principal or call the police." she offered for the umpteenth time.

"No, Mom. I've got this handled." She said, gripping a paper towel to the gashes on her forearm.

4. Childhood's End

The weekend finally arrived, and the Blood Banshee was tired of his games. He had learned by listening to their conversations that they were planning a sleepover.

Each girl told their parents they were staying at a friend's. They really intended to camp out. They figured the creature was coming out of the mirrors. They would go where there weren't any.

They had a usual spot. With one large tent, they would feel that safety in numbers thing. There was a fire pit to keep warm and an old ax for chopping wood. Maybe they could get some peace.

The Blood Banshee waited at the edge of the clearing for the night to fall.

Claura, somehow, knew that the creature had used the fluorescent colors of their fear to track them in the wilderness. She was dragged along, trapped in the mind's eye of the beast, again.

It was Saturday night. She was supposed to be dreaming in bed, but her nightmares kept her moving forward through the forest. She looked out through Blood Banshee's gaze.

She could feel the mouth filled with razor-sharp death. Fountains of Saliva gushed from that orifice. Her claws flexed. She stomped towards the campsite.

"Do you hear something?" Shawnee whispered.

"Shut up!" came the order. "There's no way for it to get us here."

How wrong they were, Claura thought. Death waited just out of sight in the trees, and Claura was forced to wait right with it.

She watched the witch fire of their pheromones glowing in the distance. The dark silhouettes sitting in the firelight gave off a light show all their own.

Everchanging, she could taste the metallic sensations wrought by each patch of luminous fog. It occurred to her that Claura was able to separate the three of them by taste and smell. The flavors were maddening.

Eventually, exhaustion got the better of the three hapless girls. They climbed into the tent and curled up in their sleeping bags without even speaking to each other.

They didn't consider they would never be speaking to each other ever again.

Claura felt herself break from the cover. Her viewpoint hovered closer and closer to the campsite. The embers in the firepit were dying out, but she no longer needed light to see in the dark.

She had reached the tent and watched a talon stretch forth to grip the tent flap and tease it forward. The Blood Banshee crept in and stood over her prey.

Allowing her to savor the moment of revenge for the way they treated her, it never considered in its primitive mind she would refuse. Or maybe its malice extended to Claura, too, after all.

She would get no more time to reflect as it fell upon the sleeping girls.

Like a whirlwind of talons, claws, and teeth, they hit the sleeping bags like the blades of a woodchipper. Blood sprouted to the roof of the tent and sprayed up its walls.

Claura screamed in its mind. She was horrified by what she was being forced to witness. She was, literally, forced to take part in it.

Again and again, the great paws fell and hacked, and the Blood Banshee was roaring with delight.

Claura was only along for the ride. She was powerless to stop it. She cried out again and again. Back home, in bed, she cried out in her sleep.

Through her frenzy of distaste, she noticed the beast had spared Becky the ringleader. The reason became evident when the Blood Banshee held forth a paw and dropped the blood-soaked fire ax in her lap where she sat, screaming.

It turned, all interest lost, now that his purpose had been fulfilled.

He was not sated by his chosen food. A child had not been offered for this revenge as per the pact.

Maybe this one was a freebie. It was happy just to have ended the source of the girl's torment and, thus, his own. It carried them from the tent and into the night.

Claura woke with a shout to her mother's frantic jostling. She had been trying to wake her daughter for hours while she was thrashing and moaning in her sleep.

On Monday, when the girls didn't show up at home for school, three sets of distraught parents forced the police to organize a search.

They would never have guessed what they found.

They came across Becky sitting by the cold fire pit, ax in hand like she was on the lookout for an assailant. She was covered in blood. The dismembered bodies of her two friends were splashed all up the insides of their tent.

Becky wouldn't manage to say anything the whole way to the emergency room, not during her trial, not even after her arrival at Torrance State Hospital.

She remained there as a mental patient in maximum security for the rest of her life.

The only sound she ever made was screaming at the top of her lungs, and then only on nights when someone there disappeared mysteriously. There was no way of implicating her locked up as she was. She just rubbed the scars on her forearm and crouched, rocking in the corner.

Time went by, and life returned to normal in Beccaria.

Then, one day, Claura noticed the family on the corner at the end of Elizabeth Street were not out tending their yard and working on their flower beds.

She hadn't had any of those nightmares lately, but she felt the cuts on her arm burning. On that night, Junior the dog barked at the front window, then, with a whimper, ran to his corner for one hour. He then returned to his vigil and barked again for a while before being hushed.

Weeks went by, and her end of the street was feeling lonelier than ever. Claura thought they might have gone on vacation or something. They seemed like they could afford to.

Winter came, and Santa brought the house a realtor's sign for Christmas.

Part Three
Missing Persons

April 2008
Edmond, West Virginia
Gillcrest Motel

Room 12

Spring might have come to West Virginia, but the night was wintery cold.

The lonely motel was an out-of-the-way sort of establishment. Such places were necessary for less than wholesome practices to take place.

There exist varying degrees of behavior that correspond to certain needs. The more dark one's depraved desire or more desperate the need, the more disreputable the behavior.

Discretion, itself, knows no limits in theory. While it may be easily obtained, its maintenance proves more difficult. Once it's given away, there's no getting it back.

As for unsavory practices, the means are often violent, and the ends no less messy.

The Blood Banshee's greatest advantage was that it never left a trace.

The motel made a great deal extra on the side for its discretion. Mysterious events and impropriety were its coin in trade, but lately, something had fallen in their lap, and the fringe benefit of covering for it was the biggest payoff yet.

Still, some things were better not advertised.

Donald Pruitt was a tax attorney working freelance for the past fifteen years. He had caught his wife cheating and was, now, in the middle of a very messy divorce.

She had a good lawyer. Hell, she sure knew how good he was in bed! There was a real threat that he might get her awarded everything and strip Donald of all he had worked for. He'd be damned if they got his dignity.

It was Donald's desire for revenge that dictated his behavior. It had very little to do with the need to care for their daughter. Their darling Vera wasn't given a say in the matter.

She loved her Daddy and all the presents he gave her. She didn't like mommy; she was always mean or her new 'boyfriend.'

Donald picked her up from school with a bag of her belongings in the back seat.

"We're taking a little trip, princess," was all the coaxing she needed. She was, after all, only seven.

Across the state line and stopping at the first dive he could find, he had gotten her McDonald's—what a treat!—and put on the TV and let it do its magic.

He closed the curtains on the darkness and turned his back on everything he knew.

He knew he had no house to go back to. The bitch had taken that.

He knew that all his belongings had been sold or pawned, converted to cash. He had done that himself.

He knew the car parked outside could not be traced to him. The motel would have no record of his real name. He was as good as gone.

Let her try to find her precious daughter. It was twenty minutes to the interstate and twenty hours to Florida. His grandparents had owned a condo right off the beach. Sylvia didn't know about it. It was in his mother's maiden name.

He forced a sigh of relief he didn't really feel. Donald had always been the meek one. He never took any chances. Isn't that what Sylvia always said?

This time he took revenge. He wished he could see her meltdown. That would have made up, some, for what she had done to him.

Pocahontas was on the television. Vera was dropping off to sleep. He snuck the bottle of vodka in its little paper bag into the bathroom to sit on the toilet. He needed some peace.

In here, maybe his little girl wouldn't be able to hear her Daddy cry.

He thought of her as all he had left. Sylvia wasn't going to take her away from him. No one can.

He stood up to the sink to wash his face. He bent down to splash double hands full of water into his eyes and over his nose. Wiping his eyes clear, he looked up into the mirror, expecting to look himself in the eyes and do some soul searching. It wasn't his face looking back at him.

What he saw was an abomination.

A blue-faced devil of scales and gnashing teeth looked back at him with enormous yellow eyes. Its head was huge, the shoulders broad, hunched over beneath a white bed sheet like a ghost. Was that a wicked smile?

Donald stood there with a look of open shock on his, otherwise dull face. His mouth worked uselessly. Before he could utter a sound, he was flung backward through the shower curtain and toppled into the tub.

He had hit his head pretty good and held it in both hands, cursing the pain. When he looked up, he expected to find it was all his imagination. But isn't that the other thing Sylvia always said he never had?

The creature looked down on him from inside the wall above the bathroom sink. It grinned its evil grin at him. Then it made for its door. The door in the mirror?

It took only a moment for Donald to register where it was headed. He climbed painfully from the tub and ran into the room, calling Vera's name.

It was too late.

The Blood Banshee already had his daughter. He could clearly see it standing just inside the big mirror in the motel room proper. It had his little girl cradled in its arms.

The man ran forward. He could see him just outside the glass, hammering his pathetic little fists. He allowed him to see his daughter alive one last time.

Offering her up towards the impotent human, it appeared as if he would give her back. Not likely!

Opening his mouth impossibly wide, he sank his fangs into the sleeping girl's throat. She came to at the last moment, but she didn't stand a chance.

In the time it took for her to utter one gurgle, the Blood Banshee had drained her dry. He held her doll form up with his claws under her arms, facing her father.

Her throat was detaching as she struggled to raise her head. Through drooping eyelids, she saw her father pounding on the window, trying to reach her. Then everything went black.

Only when the life had left her puny little body did he open the way for the screaming man. He promptly fell through the opening into the outer realm.

His last view before he died was a close-up of two blue-clawed feet. One raised up. It came thundering down and, in one blow, smashed his head in a splash of gore.

The management would claim to address any noise. They would dispose of the hapless victims' belongings. They got the most money from selling the car, just like all the other ones.

JUNE 2008

Room 17

After she was done fussing with her children, Audrey Perkins gave them one last tuck and a kiss on the forehead, each, before heading for the door.

Mona and Frederick were seven and nine. They had shared the same room for most of their lives, just not away from home in a strange hotel.

It was seedy looking, as far as cheap motels go. It was the only room left in town. Robert Perkins had wanted to drive further, but the hour was late.

The second time the tires headed off the pavement, Audrey had demanded he find them a hotel. After all, Mammoth Cave had lain beneath the Kentucky landscape for millions of years. It would still be there in the morning.

He was a lump under the covers when she returned from the room next door.

Staring down at his unmoving form by the light of the television set, she wished again there was a connecting door between rooms. She had been up since dawn, herself. A tremendous yawn rocked her slight frame.

Her head had not reached the pillow when she heard a thump from the children's room. She laid back and gave it a four-count.

The noise was repeated twice more, and she heard a faint yell. From her daughter.

She was up like a flash and called out as she ran for the door.

"Robert! Robert? Didn't you hear that?! Robert, Get up! I think the kids are in trouble."

She just knew this place was dangerous, just from the look of it!

She fumbled the key around the opening in the lock until she found it, wrenched at the knob, and burst in the door.

The bathroom light was left on with the door cracked. It did nothing to light the darkness beyond. It obscured her view.

She could have sworn she saw a large, white shape cross the room like someone big wearing a king-sized sheet. It glided from the children's side of the room toward the wall.

It must have been a trick of the light.

Jesus, GOD!!! Let it have been caused by the light in her eyes!

She scrabbled for the light switch, calling into the dark.

"Freddy? Mona! Answer Mommy!"

Managing, at last, to turn the light on, she saw the reason they had not answered.

They were not there.

Desperately she dug through every corner of the room, under the bed, behind the sofa chair. Only the rumpled blankets gave any sign they had ever been there.

Audrey Perkins wailed incoherently. Screaming for her husband, she dashed back to their room.

"Robert, for the Love of GOD! WAKE UP!"

Reaching his side of the bed, she shook at his inert form. She pulled back a hand covered in his blood.

The other hand pressed to her mouth in mute horror; she used the bloody hand to yank back the sheet and blanket. What she saw made her faint: his entire neck looked like it had been gnawed off by a tiger.

There wasn't a drop of blood.

When she came to, she was being held somewhere dark.

She could hear her children moaning. They were being dragged closer by the fiendish thing that wore the bedsheet.

She was unable to see what held her hands up towards the ceiling. It was utterly dark.

As the creature stepped into view, it glowed in the dark, illuminating their surroundings.

It was a torture chamber.

The Blood Banshee stepped in through the wall-length mirror and dumped her children next to their father's corpse. He was fully prepared, now, to enjoy himself for days—maybe weeks—depending on how long they could withstand it.

Room 21

Twenty-one was her lucky number. Then she turned twenty-two. June had lived in room twenty-one for six years. That was when Stu, the manager of the Gillcrest, had wooed her away from her ma.

It was fancy to have her own place. She was fed and paid money. Stu even gave her a credit card to shop for clothes. She could come and go as she pleased. The better to show off her wares and attract more men.

Stu showered her with jewelry and even gave her a hot new car. He made sure she knew who took care of her and to always come home. That's where he wanted her man friends to come. Room twenty-one. The room in the back.

It was the only room to let in the motel that faced the woods in the back. It was a gorgeous view and all hers.

All she had to do in return for all of this was entertain half the county and any callers from out of town.

The frequent callers would only stay the short while it took to get done with their business. It kept her privacy.

All of this became hers when she was only sixteen.

Stu was the only one who didn't have to pay. He used to come to her once or twice a day when she was young.

When she turned eighteen, she was allowed in the bar at the center of town.

Starvin' Marvin's was the local hangout for everyone from the construction crews to factory workers and all the townsfolk in between.

It made a perfect place to find clients for her liaisons. It was only a thirty-foot walk from the motel.

Stu even gave her a fake I.D. for her eighteenth birthday so guys could buy her drinks.

She liked the way she was treated. She felt like the Queen of Farmville. Then she got older. She could tell she was getting older because Stu used her less and less each year.

When she turned twenty, he began making reasons to complain. By the time she was at the end of her sixth year of work, Stu was beating her.

It got its worst when Stu found out she was pregnant.

Her business was notably lacking. Only a few went in for that sort of thing once she really started to show.

June didn't think it could get any worse. Then, her twenty-second birthday was coming around, and it was the same day as her due date.

Stu had forbidden her to see a doctor. He didn't want any record at all of the pregnancy.

Early on, she had thought Stu would take her to get an abortion. As the third month came and went, she stirred up the courage to ask. He flew into a rage and threatened to kill her himself before letting her go to a clinic.

Now, there was a knock at her door, the first in ages.

"Juney, honey?" she heard Stu's voice drawl. "How are you doin' in there?"

Truthfully, her cramps had been something awful. She felt like she had to take a dump all the time, and the baby was really kicking.

In fact, anytime she came near a mirror, the infant's movements felt like it was fixing to tear right out of her.

"I'm fine," she answered though she felt like anything but.

He used his key to open the door.

"No!" she stepped forward to block the door too late. Halfway through her first step, she doubled over in pain.

"I figured it was time." He said, taking her up by the arm. "You need to come with me right away!"

The excited tone of his voice reassured her for the moment.

She couldn't see straight. The pain was coming in waves as he hefted one of her arms over his shoulder. He half dragged her around the other side of the main building. Her feet wouldn't work.

He put her down to open the double doors that were set on the ground.

"What is this?" she gasped. "A cellar?"

She could barely speak between contractions.

He was like the picture of an expectant father.

"I just need you to hold on a little longer." She felt like she should say something.

"Stu," she stammered. "The father, he's…"

Stu wouldn't let her finish what she was going to say. He didn't like where it was going.

He was nothing like those Dads he watched coming through here. Stu watched them on his hidden cameras.

He liked to keep a set of tapes from the more juicy encounters. June's tapes had filled a nearby adult video store's shelves for years.

He never shared any of the profits with her. He knew one day she'd outlive her usefulness. He was glad it was sooner than later. She wasn't the first, and she really wasn't the best.

What she had been was the youngest. Now those days were over, and she had to be disposed of.

That was gonna be great fodder for the other set of tapes he'd started. He had cameras everywhere. He'd known about his unpaying tenant for quite some time now.

He figured the creature, whatever it was, would be hopelessly drawn to Juney's swollen body. It seemed to like children best. That would take care of her.

Then he could get down to the business of finding a new whore for room twenty-one.

June struggled as he dragged her by her wrists down the slick steps. "NO! Where are you taking me?!"

"I'm taking you to your just desserts!"

Stu was getting excited, and a maniacal gleam entered his eyes she had never seen before. "You see? You're providing the meal, and I'm sure the rest of you will just be dessert! GET IT???"

June certainly did not. She didn't want to. How could she accept that, after all the royal treatment, this was how it was gonna end?

Across the basement was a well-ventilated room with a wall-length mirror. Reflected in it were the torture implements that a certain select clientele had enjoyed since his grandpappy ran this place.

Stu dragged the pregnant June to the center of the room. She stared around herself in horror.

"How, the Hell long has THIS been here?"

She squealed. It was sick and perverted. She wanted to look at him like he was just a depraved child. It got harder as he shackled her wrists and jerked them viciously to the ceiling.

Stu only responded by slapping her hard. Ripping her dirty white shirt off and her little panties, he thrust his face in her's and squealed once, real loud, like a pig.

"DINGLE LINGLE LING!" he screeched in her face. He must have lost it.

"COME and GET IT!" Then it dawned on her what her fate was.

She dangled, naked, facing the looking glass wall. She could see it clear as day, standing in the mirror. It had appeared out of nowhere. It studied her, looking her up and down.

June was shaking her head violently.

"No, no no no no…NO!" She couldn't take her eyes off it. It just stood there with its paws by its sides, obscured by a death shroud. It looked back and forth between her and Stu.

It turned to her reflection. She could see herself with her arms up high, feet struggling on tiptoes—her belly full and swollen beyond belief. The ghost creature turned its hood towards her and reached one blue claw to her reflection's belly.

Like that, it was next to her! It was breathing in her face. Its scaly claw was stroking her belly lovingly. June screamed.

The Blood Banshee was pleased with this offering. He drooled as he looked forward to crouching down between the girl's legs and gobbling the newborn as it exited her birth canal. So fresh!

It was its due, after all, for the pathetic human had profited from his presence.

If only he weren't so foolish to have recorded its comings and goings. Look at him now. The wicked little man was still in the room! The temerity! Did he have no concept of the position he was in?

The depraved human wanted to watch.

At least he wasn't on his knees, like the weaklings from eons in the past. Someone always thought worshipping the Blood Banshee was useful, like all those ancient sycophants to their uncaring Gods. He had no cult, needed no followers. He was an engine of destruction, clear and simple.

This man will learn. Right now.

Stu thought he was safe, like harboring the monster and keeping its secret should be rewarded. He watched as the Beast turned and grabbed him by both shoulders, dragging him into an embrace. It sank its fangs into his neck.

June got the final satisfaction of watching the look on Stu's face change to shock over the creature's shrouded shoulder. Then the last wave of childbirth hit her like a freight train.

She screamed in agony again and again. Insanity gripped her, bulging her eyes. It drew her lips up into impossible laughter, as dropping Stu's body to the floor, the beast returned his attention to her.

The bloody feast was the first like it he had enjoyed in a long, long time.

The Blood Banshee knew it was time to move on. Leaving the cadaverous vault through the mirrored wall, he emerged from the mirror on the back of the manager's office door.

Moving to the cabinet that housed the hidden camera feeds, he found every single tape that included his presence.

In the end, he simply stepped back out and left the hoard behind the playroom wall. It amused him to think of watching them, himself, someday.

This modern technology presented a problem not faced in the millions of years of his existence. He would have to bear it in mind.

It was morning by the time he emerged behind a young couple and their two children as they checked out from their room.

Scuttling after them within the side mirror of their SUV, he ascertained they were headed west.

"Well, we have a long way to go, kids," The father said. "We won't be stopping until we reach Missouri, so I hope you all went to the bathroom."

"Yes, Dad." the children chorused.

"California, here we come!" their mom cheered.

April 2009
I-40 Westbound
The Doyle Family of Four

Thursday 10:20 am

"Stop touching me! Mom!" Jennifer yelled again.

"I wasn't!" Ronny pleaded.

"Ronny, keep your hands to yourself, for the last time." their mother said.

"Ophelia, they're kids. We knew it was going to be like this." Nick Doyle said to his wife.

They had been on the road for two days already. He didn't expect tensions to start running high so soon. After that last stop at the dirty motel, though, things had gone sour.

Comic books didn't occupy his nine-year-old son, Ronald, well enough from the sound of things back there. His seven-year-old sister, Jennifer, was complaining when she wasn't totally withdrawn. It wasn't like her.

And every time he looked at the road, he kept seeing someone out of the corner of his eye through the rearview mirror.

It was like someone covered in a sheet was riding in the third-row seat behind the children. But, every time he tried to look up at the mirror, there was nothing there.

"What's wrong, dear?" his wife asked.

"Nothing," he replied. He had no concrete reason to alarm her, so he kept it to himself. Still, the distraction was putting a damper on their vacation.

He couldn't get over the uneasy feeling that they weren't alone.

The Blood Banshee rode in the vehicle and tried to relax. His last meal should sustain him indefinitely. Being so close to the two children like this was tantalizing.

Their heady aroma filled his nostrils. Their whining voices entertained him. The fact that they unaware of his scrutiny amused him. The desire to feed on this family and his willingness to see how far he could travel in this manner warred within him.

In the end, he occupied himself with pinching the girl just to hear her squeal. She blamed the boy to his advantage.

He wondered how long he could keep this up.

Thursday 3:45 pm

The McDonald's beside the interstate was packed. The Doyles had stopped for a meal and refreshments. While they looked up at the menu boards, The Blood Banshee appraised the crowd from behind them.

He was waiting for someone who would serve him, as well.

"What are you having?" Nick asked his wife.

"I don't know. What are you having?"

He hated when she did that.

"How about you kids? What would you like in your happy meals?"

"I'll have chicken nuggets," Ronny said.

"Can I have a cheeseburger with only ketchup?" Jennifer asked.

They had reached the counter through the crowd of waiting customers with their receipts in hand.

"I'll have a number one."

The unsuspecting family was enjoying their processed meat when the Blood Banshee saw his meal walking into the restroom.

A little boy was entering to relieve himself unaccompanied by any adults. There was no one else in the tiny facilities when the fiend moved up behind the full-size mirror on the wall. The boy went to walk past and was snatched from existence.

The Blood Banshee had just enough time to drink his blood and consume his flesh before returning to the Doyle family's vehicle before they could leave without him.

He left the chewed-up remains of the boy's bloodless corpse just out of sight through the restroom mirror.

By the time the missing child's parents could raise the alarm, the Doyles were five miles down the interstate.

"I have to find a hotel. It's getting dark." Nick was not looking forward to another dingy, overnight stay. They were somewhere in New Mexico, and the land was flat and filled with scrub to either side. They hadn't seen another car in either direction for hours.

"I told you we should have flown," Audrey said for the thousandth time.

Ronny and Jennifer were actually pulling each other's hair in the seat behind.

"Did NOT! You did it first!" they both screeched back and forth. Their mother had given up trying to intervene.

Nick had stopped looking in the rearview at them after the last glimpse of the phantom rider in the third-row seat. Its face was blue, and it was covered in a white sheet. It grinned its razor teeth at him.

The Blood Banshee had decided he'd had enough of this family. From the reflected world, he punched through the floorboard of the vehicle and tore a hole in the fuel line. The engine coughed and sputtered out.

"I can't believe it!" Nick exclaimed. "What is happening, now?!" He got it over to the side and put on the flashers as it crept to a stop.

"We should have enough gas to get to the next town!" Nick complained.

"I guess I'll have to walk and get some." Truthfully, he was relieved to get some time away from all the ruckus.

Four hours later, he returned to an empty car. There was no sign of his family. Only the wicked beast that stood behind his reflection in the car window.

It was the last thing he saw as it reached for him.

Suddenly, it was like he was looking out the car window at the place he was just standing. He tried to turn, but he was held in place.

Someone was tearing his head off.

It didn't take long after consuming the last family that he was able to 'hitch' a ride from a passing semi.

The truck driver passed the car that was on the shoulder. Was someone standing by it wrapped in a white blanket? He could have sworn someone was illuminated by the car's four ways.

He did see a person thereafter he went by. He clearly saw the ghostly figure, but in the next flash of the hazard lights, they'd vanished.

From that glimpse in the side mirror, the Blood Banshee moved into the passing truck. In the reversed image of the cab, he sat in the passenger seat, invisible.

The driver only registered a brief uneasy feeling every time he looked in the passenger side mirror while the Blood Banshee enjoyed the reflection of himself grinning evilly from inside the window.

From his angle, the driver could not see that reflection. He had no idea anyone was even there.

The southwestern night rushed by.

May 2009
Albuquerque, New Mexico
Walmart Supercenter

The endless canyons of clothing racks towered around the child as he wandered off from his mother again, bored.

"Pablo," she called again from the top she was inspecting.

"No deambularen, otra vez." She wasn't even looking this time.

Pablo found himself looking up at the full-length mirror around the corner from the dressing room. What looked back at him was not his reflection.

It was huge, draped in white and scaled blue. Yellow, hungry eyes poked at him from beneath its hood.

Before Pablo had time to react, its blue paws shot out from the mirror, dragging him inside.

In its devilish embrace, not a sound escaped alerting the boy's mother of his disappearance.

Overnight, this Walmart had increased its number of child abductions it had been covering up almost tenfold.

August 2012
Scottsdale, Arizona
Odyssey in The Desert
The Mirror Maze

It was past closing time. The teenage couples had snuck in to see the place at night.

Bobby Warner, his girlfriend Sarah Hess, and his best friend, Jake Chandler, and his girl, Samantha Brooks, wandered the darkness near the control room. Flashlight beams crossed and spun crazily.

Bobby got out his key. He had worked the morning shift and kept his key instead of turning it in that day.

"I'm telling you guys," he was saying. "There's something going on lately that they've been covering up."

Jake wasn't buying it. He was just into fooling around with Sam in any location available. This place was gonna be more exciting than most, especially without all the little kids running all over the place.

"They can't do that. Word would have gotten out." Jake said.

"Really," said Sam. "How many kids did you say went missing?"

"Twelve. And that was only last month. In just one month, I mean, Jesus!"

"Altogether, it's been, like thirty kids that I know of. Their parents come in and are like, 'excuse me, we can't find our child,' and the tears start." Bobby was really broken up over it. Sarah placed a hand on his arm in concern.

"It's not your fault, baby." She truly loved Bobby. When he got the job, just a janitor's position, he was so stoked. When he showed her around the Mirror Maze, it had been wonderful. It was a magical memory that she would cherish forever.

Now, the place was cold and dark like a tomb. They stood beside a hidden door.

Samantha watched him choose the key for the control room. "Do they have cameras?" she asked.

"Yeah, I think so," Bobby answered. "If the monitors are anywhere, they'd be in the security office. That's the one room they don't let me clean."

Once inside the control room, he reached for the simple bank of switches and turned them all on.

Outside, the Mirror Maze came to life. Ultraviolet lighting struck the halls painted in dazzling colors. Ornate frameworks of scrolling vines intertwined in concentric archways. A nighttime fairyland of endless tunnels extended in all directions.

The girls looked around in amazement. Their hair was lit up in pasty hues. Their eyes were purple. Their teeth shone, mouths glowing, open in childlike wonder.

"This way," Bobby said. "The security office is on the other side of the Mayan temple, but you need to stay close."

Jake wasn't listening. Samantha was leading him by the hand, but he was being led more by his hormones. He was hoping for a place he could stop and get her alone.

Sarah was close to Bobby, hand in hand. She couldn't help feeling the magic of her surroundings despite their grim mission.

"This place is so beautiful!" she sighed.

Bobby didn't say a word. He was concentrating on where they were going. It was easy to get lost in this place. He'd only been working here for a few weeks and still had trouble navigating it.

It was a maze, after all. The tantalizing effects of the countless mirrors only added to his difficulty.

"Look at that!" Samantha said. An orange butterfly glowed near the ceiling. "It's a Monarch." She gripped Jake's hand.

"Come on," she pulled him in its direction. "Let's follow it."

It bobbed and weaved, realistically, as it flittered down the hall. It turned an entirely different direction. In two turns, they were lost from sight.

Bobby and Sarah were moving through the Mayan portion of the maze. Stylized walls in bright orange colors made her feel like she really was in a tomb now. Or the scene from a horror movie. She felt goosebumps as she imagined a mummy lurching around the bend after her, arms open wide to catch her.

She had no idea how close to the truth she was.

Bobby was the model of tension. Like a hunting dog, he was alert and fixed on their trail. He kept looking from side to side as if he expected something really would jump out at them.

It was really making her nervous.

"Here it is."

They had stopped in front of a door near the emergency exit. He chose the key and fumbled it at the lock. That was when Sarah looked behind her.

"Where did Jake and Sam go?"

Bobby stopped dead. He spun with a jerk.

"What?! Oh no…"

He renewed his efforts on the door, grasped the handle, and rushed inside. He pulled Sarah in behind him, not too gently.

"Hey!"

"I'm sorry, babe." He was apologizing, but he was in a hurry to check the camera monitors. He just knew there was something wrong.

He turned them on. Screen after screen showed dim images of the halls. In black and white, the walls not only lost their color they also lost most of their definition. The cameras weren't meant to photograph in an ultraviolet light source.

He searched the grainy images until he found a screen his friends were in. He hoped it wasn't too late, but he didn't even know for what.

"Keep checking the monitors," he ordered. He needed to check for something else.

Sarah struggled with the controls and did her best to learn the settings and layout as fast as she could. There were hundreds of images spread throughout fifty monitors, and they all looked alike.

Bobby, in the meantime, had located the library of previous video footage. He had memorized the dates and times of the disappearances that he knew of.

This was his one chance to get to the bottom of this. If there was something perverted going on, he was gonna go to the authorities with some evidence.

Meanwhile, Samantha and Jake were hopelessly lost. The painted forest had lost its magic. Jake had become more insistent on getting his hands all over her, and it was annoying.

"COME on, babe..." he breathed in her ear. He continued groping her persistently, unwilling to discontinue the kisses he showered on her. "Just get into the magic of this place."

But she felt like something was wrong. She broke free of him.

"Stop it!" She pushed him off her with a shout.

He was about to get mad at her and lunge back with an accusation. As he opened a mouth set in a petulant look of anger, that's when it happened.

The black lights shut off with an echoing 'SHUNK.'

The lovers were suspended in darkness. Then the emergency lighting came up, red and raw, bathing the halls in the color of blood.

As if that wasn't bad, voices began muttering from all directions. As they rose in volume, Samantha covered her ears in horror.

They were children's voices.

"What the FUCK is going ON!" shouted Jake. Around and around, he turned in place. The actions of a caged beast made him look like a child himself.

"Who's there!" he yelled with false bravado. His voice cracked in animal terror. "I'm warning you!"

Great idea. Yell at the haunted house. Samantha would have laughed if she didn't feel like it was the end of the world.

"What is happening!" she shrieked. "What do you want from us?!" The voices had taken on a chant.

One by one, they took it up.

"Blood. Blood. BLOOD!!!"

Then they appeared before the terror-stricken teenagers. In each mirror, one by one, thirty dismembered children stood to surround them. Everything was lit up as red as the inside of a fresh corpse.

And corpses were what these children were. Animated by their agony or the evil intent that fueled their mutual destruction, they reached out within the mirrors. They were reflections of things that weren't even there.

Jake and Sam held one another, sobbing. They crouched in each other's arms in the center of the circle.

As one, the children stepped out of the mirrors.

Bobby found the first roll that held the feeds of the day, three days before, when a little girl had gone missing.

Rose Tyler was seven when her school brought her, along with eighty-nine other children on a packed yellow bus, to see the Mirror Maze. She didn't return to the bus.

Bobby meant to find out what happened to her.

He plugged the reel into the apparatus then ran it on a specialized screen with multiple outputs. Six separate images representing different camera feeds had recorded simultaneously. By clicking buttons for each feed, he could switch through subsequent groups of feeds. He sifted through them all until he came across the one with the girl with a big bow in her hair.

He remembered her by that bow. When her parents began circulating the last photo taken of her, that had stuck out. At least it had for him.

He didn't even recall the police ever coming to investigate. In the last month, the toll had reached thirty. Thirty cases that no one managed to come up to inspect in person.

He knew the City Council had a lot of money invested in this place. It brought in business from around the world. If it ever got out that it was a bottomless pit, a trap for the occasional child, they could call it the Eighth Wonder of the frickin' World. No parent was going to risk their child being sucked away here.

It took a while, but he found her. The bow and the little ponytail bobbed and weaved its silhouette through the grainy rainforest as she chased the butterfly. Her shadowy form obscured the wall paintings as he followed her from feed to feed.

He eventually came to her final feed. She was in a hall all by herself. Some glitch in the system or trick of the reflections had led her, somehow, down a corridor that shouldn't be there.

The camera panned, and she was out of the frame for a few seconds. It panned back, and she was clearly seen in profile, her reflection on the other side from the camera in a mirror she was standing next to.

The camera panned again. Then it panned back.

Rose was still there, looking up as if she were face to face with someone tall. He watched her reach up an exploring hand as if she were going to uncover something.

Bobby couldn't tell at first what was wrong with this picture. He saw right before the camera could pan away. He paused it just to get a longer look.

What he saw made him call Sarah. She had to see this too. He had to be sure he wasn't crazy.

"Sarah? Come look at this."

"What is it?"

"This is the little girl I told you about. Remember when I said I recognized the bow in her hair from the parents' photo of her?" He pointed at her on the screen. "What do you see?"

"I see the little girl standing in the mirror frame. So what?"

Bobby rewinded it couple of seconds.

"See here?" He pointed at the girl standing next to her reflection. The camera panned away. "Now watch."

The camera panned back. There she stood reflected in the mirror, but the real her was gone.

There was only the reflection reaching up. Then the camera panned away one last time.

By the time the view panned back, she had completely disappeared.

"Where'd she go?" Sarah gasped.

Bobby rewound it. "See here? She's stepping forward."

"But she's facing a mirror!" Sarah noted.

"It's a side view," Bobby said. "You can't see what she's looking at if it's a reflection or not. Clearly, she's facing the wall."

"But then, she just vanishes. There's no view of her coming out."

"See if you can find another one. Another disappearing child."

They went through three other reels dated for the days the three other children Bobby memorized information about had disappeared. He had been looking forward to catching some sleazy guy on camera walking off with someone else's kid. He was unprepared for what he was finding.

"There!" Sarah said, pointing at the screen. "He walked into the wall. Or where a wall SHOULD have been."

"That's crazy. It can't be. That would mean they're all still in there!"

"It looks like they were all talking to someone," Sarah noted. "But the angle is bad. You can't see who it is."

"What's behind the mirrors, anyway?"

"Nothing. Just a solid wall. And how do you explain them disappearing before their reflections?"

"Wait a minute." Sarah just remembered. "Where's Jake and Sam?"

Jake had Sam by the hand. They were running as fast as they could through the reddened maze.

Everywhere they turned, there was a dead child reaching for them.

They slammed into a wall at top speed. They had reached a dead end.

They turned to go back, but somehow it was closed off by a pane of glass. They were boxed in, but how?

They tried in every direction. It was no use. They were in a mirrored room that was only ten feet square. The way they had come in was blocked. It was the only wall they had come across that they could see through. What did that mean?

Something was nagging at Jake's scared mind. He almost had a grasp on what it was. Then he looked out through the glass and saw his reflection a little way down the corridor.

"Hey, look," he said, pointing. Samantha gave up pounding on the glass as well.

They stared at their reflections until it dawned on them what they were seeing.

They were trapped INSIDE the mirror!

Bobby found his friends. They had almost made it to the security office. They were right outside the end of the rainforest.

The angle was bad, but Bobby could see them clearly on the screen pounding on the glass wall they were stuck behind.

"That's impossible!" Sarah cried. "That's a mirror. They are inside the mirror!"

"Stay here," Bobby ordered. "I'm gonna go see."

Sarah followed him on the monitors as he made his way to his friends. It wasn't far.

From the moment he stepped out of the office, he was gripped with fear.

Everything was lit up the color of blood. Someone had turned on the emergency lighting.

He took two more turns and came upon them. Jake and Samantha were pounding on the inside of the wall, looking out at him. He could barely hear them shouting.

Bobby's reflection turned the corner behind them as he did. He walked forward, and so did his reflection. There were three of them now as he reached up to touch the glass. His hand and that of his reflection met as he touched the surface of the glass.

Over his reflection's shoulder, he saw a corridor of reflections in the corner glass extending off into eternity.

Down the long hall of this optical illusion stood a shadowy figure. It was draped in white like a bedsheet ghost. Its face was lost in the shadow of its hood.

It approached them from behind. Bobby looked behind him and saw there was nothing there. This thing was stepping out through distant dimensions of reflected light. It was heading right for his unsuspecting friends. He had no choice but to back away from the glass, or it would get him, too.

The only problem was, the more he stepped back, the closer that brought his reflection right to it!

It lifted an arm, reaching a talon towards his back. He had to run. He had to get his reflection around the corner before that creep caught up to it.

He turned to run and came face to face with a nightmare.

Under the white hood, lit up blood-red in the emergency lights, was a face straight out of Hell. Scales and cadaverous cheekbones framed the bulging eyes and gaping mouth of a demon. It was the drooling fangs that held Bobby's attention as the thing held him, now.

He strained to turn his head. He could see Jake and Sarah were now behind him.

That's how it worked. As soon as this thing touched you, you were switched with your reflection.

It was too bad he would never escape with that information.

Sarah watched in horror as Bobby stepped back from the mirror their friends were trapped behind. He was turning to run. He smacked into the hooded figure as it appeared out of nowhere behind him.

"Nooooo!'" Sarah screamed.

It was too late. The thing wrapped her boyfriend in its black embrace.

They both vanished.

All she could do was watch, helplessly, as Jake and Sam were lost from view. Buckets of red began splashing on the inside of the glass until the entire surface was covered in her best friends' blood.

Then, before her very eyes, the glass became a mirror again. Spattered blood gave way to empty reflection. The contents within faded and were lost forever.

Sarah could only watch the monitors. Her misery and terror were all she had left. Her friends were dead. Bobby was dead. With no idea of what she should do, what was meaningful in her life, she stood in the security office, alone. She continued to face the monitors, favoring them with her blank-eyed stare.

The power went out. She stood in darkness. Turning her head from side to side, she looked about in confusion. The emergency lighting came on, shedding a dull yellow glow on the control panels. She could see her dim reflection was distorted by their curved surface. Backlit by the amber watch lights, Sarah's face was lost in shadow.

Her lone silhouette was overcome by another. Slowly rising up behind her reflection, the intruder emerged from the shadows. It had gotten in the room but did not come through the door.

She watched in horror as the thing towered over her reflection before slowly turning her head.

She had to see if there was something really behind her.

She was struck by the horror of looking straight in the face of madness. Its lunatic gaze bored holes deep into the fear center of her mind.

She couldn't take her eyes off the nest of fangs as they drew closer and closer to her face. Ropes of drool rinsed at the layers of red spattered around its mouth. She could smell the blood on its breath.

Her friends' blood.

She began to scream.

Part Four
The Haunting

Chapter 1
Bride of The Blood Banshee
Introduction

Claura Roberts had grown up. She didn't have the benefit of a rich Daddy or a stable home to nurture her, but she thought she turned out okay. She'd managed to stay out of therapy. She had never wound up in an institution or jail. Or rehab.

Over the course of her young adult life, she had kept a string of jobs. Waitress and cashier might be representative of the few jobs that could grace her resume at first. But she kept herself fed and stayed clean, more so than could be said for even those who were well-to-do.

And if she never laid down roots, it was because she enjoyed staying on the move.

She got caught up in modeling for a time. It began with more unsavory venues until she eventually broke out more mainstream, retaining a bad-girl kind of image. Then she crossed over to the other side of the camera.

Photography became a passion for a good period of her youth. She worked her way through the colleges she had saved up for as a model and even obtained a degree in journalism. That was a dog-eat-dog world, so she joined the military.

As a combat photographer, she received the best training in warfare and field techniques. It was invigorating and educational, steeping her into a lifestyle she found useful for her ultimate goal.

She had never stopped tracking the whereabouts of the Blood Banshee.

Growing up in a solitary existence kept her situation from becoming known. Men had trouble equating her tough-girl persona with the shy aloofness she seemed to show. They could never accept her inability to get close for very long, and it suited her well. Sharing her bed would mean someone would question her about the nightmares.

That would prove counterproductive to the mission. And she was on a mission.

Winter 2007 had hit Beccaria like a wrecking ball.

The record snowfall, obnoxious as it was, managed to brighten the landscape. It made going places even more problematic, though. With nowhere to go in the first place, the Internet was Claura's only salvation.

She followed the rash of mysterious disappearances showing up on the news websites. From town to town, it leads a gradual trail further away from Beccaria.

It seemed like only she could see the pattern.

Claura had quickly learned the correlation between the incidents—hints and allegations mostly, and her nightly forays with the killer fiend. She retained the ability to share what it sensed; sights, sounds, and smells whenever she dreamed. Or, at least, when it was on the hunt.

Some nights, she would find that she could sleep in peace. Then there were nights that the Blood Banshee was killing. Those nights, for Claura, were truly awful, bordering on traumatizing.

Her mother never would understand. She only found an expedient explanation to satisfy herself, and Claura did not disabuse her of that. After all, the events that year would be enough to give any child nightmares.

The murders perpetrated by Claura's fellow classmate had been the talk of the town, a town that they had gained actual access to, now, if not complete acceptance.

There was something about a senseless rampage by one of your own to make outsiders seem less threatening.

Where there was once a dismissal, now there was an acknowledgment of guilt, silent as it was. They wouldn't openly apologize, just like they wouldn't discuss the 'tragedy.'

As for Claura, time wore on; the dreams became less intense as the Blood Banshee moved away from Beccaria, away from where she was.

That was a bit of a relief.

Still, she could keep tabs on it. Through erroneous news reports and what little she could glean from its surroundings in her dreams, she could pinpoint its location. She even kept an old highway map of the country where she marked its passage.

It was never idle for long, always on the move. And it never stopped killing for long.

In the meantime, Claura had painstakingly formed a back trail of the creature's activities from before her encounters with it.

It wasn't easy. She had to travel to certain towns for access to their records when the Internet let her down. She was slowly tracking down the source. Or, at least, where it first appeared.

Esoteric libraries and mythological websites yielded nothing. That was hard to believe. Had nobody ever heard of this thing before? There was no mention of it, fact or fiction. If not fact, then at least, legend.

That it didn't have a cult following to go with the slasher movie sequels was a testament to its ability to stay out of the public eye. This became more and more frustrating. With the prevalence of monster movies and paranormal thrillers, this thing would have stuck out in a league all its own. It was like a monster movie come to life, complete with the untold backstory. And there was no mistaking how ancient this thing was.

She thought she found where the present-day killings originated. A family in Connecticut had gone missing from their beds in 1994. Maybe the place warranted a visit. If she could track this thing back far enough, maybe she could find out something about it. Maybe, even, find a way to stop it, and stop it she had to do.

If for only her peace of mind and a good night's sleep, she had to try.

November 2018
Norwich, Connecticut
101 North Main Street

1. Boy Meets Girl

The house sat close to the street and was enormous. Behind a token wrought iron fence and up a tiny walkway, the boarding house towered over its quarter-acre lot, one of two dozen Lords of the Lawns that lined both sides of the tiny, little street.

A wrap-around porch girdled the big white house. It was in decent repair and had fresh tile rooftops to prevent the elements from destroying the, undoubtedly, dated interior and its furnishings.

The upper windows were perched like a pair of eyes. Claura felt like she was being scrutinized as she approached.

It was a long and difficult trail that led her to this place. Just three doors away were the house where the Mackenzies had disappeared. She could make this house her base.

After leaving the military with a pension and a head full of bad memories, she found a position as an investigative reporter for a small paranormal magazine.

The Cryptic Times made a perfect cover for the mission. Not only did it keep her comfortable financially, but it also gave her access to the research capabilities and the travel reimbursements necessary to bring the thing to the ground. She was actually on the trail of a mystery true to her magazine's content. That was a strange coincidence.

That her editors had no clue what she was really after was for her to know. They thought she was after the Slenderman or some such. A known figure or serial killer, or just an odd number of disappearances. Hell, it might be aliens! They had no clue what it was she was after.

It didn't really matter. She was confident they would approve of her findings.

Claura smiled to herself with grim humor. A breaking story of a new monster that actually existed would net, both her and the Cryptic Times, a fortune.

She just wanted to be the one to take it down.

Claura harbored no illusions that she fought for the greater good or was taking sides in the battle between good and evil. Her motivations, as far as she knew, were entirely selfish.

All she wanted was to live in peace. It's what everyone wants. For her to live the rest of her life free of nightmares in a world devoid of monsters was her driving force. It's what got her out of bed every morning. There was no room for anything or anyone else in her life.

She was on the porch, looking at the room for rent' sign as she tried the doorbell. The glass door which preceded the oak one showed her the present image of her appearance, albeit in reverse.

She avoided mirrors, naturally. She was able to affect a comfortably grungy fashion sense that didn't require much to maintain, and that was a blessing. She was presentable in public and most high-end establishments, respectively.

She had traveled far and wide in the search for cryptids—legendary creatures and was as at home in a field tent as she was in a posh hotel.

This place, she thought, giving one last look up its facade, should be right in the middle, as far as bed and breakfasts go.

At least she didn't have to worry about a cover for a change. Hostile government takeovers were far in the past. And they thought THEY were dangerous!

No. She could play this for what it was. She was on a legitimate investigation into an epidemic of disappearances. Whoever ran this place was probably here the whole time. They were bound to know something.

I wasn't hungover, for a change, when the doorbell rang. I wasn't going to care about my appearance, regardless.

Whoever it was probably didn't have any business here unless it was the kind that wouldn't keep them very long: Jehovah's Witnesses or something.

Boy, was I ever wrong?

Claura was looking up at the monster of a house when the man came to the door. Shielding her eyes from the setting sun with one hand, she was able to see him through the screen door.

She was looking at a man roughly the same age pulling his housecoat closed over himself self-consciously, running a hand through his unruly hair.

Not bad looking, she thought. Kinda soft and round on the edges.

You can bet he's needed to get out his whole life.

There was a goddess on my front lawn. With her head tipped back, taking in the house, she was the picture of a siren rising from the depths.

A dark haystack of hair framed her angelic face. A lock of blue trailed down the left side. I didn't dare look any further down for fear of getting caught.

"Can I help you?" I stammered, pulling my housecoat shut. I surreptitiously kicked my fluffy slippers off to the side.

She stepped up onto the porch. I knew my mouth was hanging open. There wasn't a damned thing I could do about it.

"Yeah. You have a room for rent?" Claura asked, pointing at the sign next to the door.

"Uh." The guy managed. "Sure!" He practically fell over himself, pushing open the screen door. "Won't you come in?"

Claura was used to this sort of reaction. After all, she'd been through; she still retained a striking image. Usually, she didn't have time for such shenanigans. There was something about this guy, though. He had a bumbling honesty she had never encountered. Her heart immediately went out to him.

"I'm Jack," he said, offering a hand. "Jack Lawrence. Welcome to Harrowing House."

"Claura Roberts. Pleased to meet you."

And she was surprised to find she truly was.

Her smile hit me like a brick. It was brief, but it lit up the sun. I could tell it wasn't a common arrangement for those perfect lips. I couldn't wait to hear them shape my name. We shook hands.

Forcing sappy thoughts from my head, I led her into the bottom floor parlor.

"Can I get you some coffee?" I asked.

"How about a beer?" Claura requested teasingly. "It's afternoon, isn't it? And I'm parched from the drive."

I saw an opening, finally. "Where were you headed from?" I inquired innocently. Smooth.

"El Paso." She replied as if that said it all.

"What brings you to these parts?" came my next question. I put on my good southern drawl. She actually giggled!

My, what a charmer, Claura thought to herself. For the first time she could remember, she didn't feel all alone. What was it about this guy? There was a sense that he was someone besieged, maybe by the same thing as her.

Sure, she had been in the trenches, fought on the front lines. He seemed like he had been surviving on life's half rations—a citizen in the town perpetually under siege.

He returned from the other room and sat in an ancient love seat across from her.

She looked into his deep, sunken eyes. There WAS something a bit hagridden there.

Their gazes met, and something tangible melted off of him just then. A warm glow suffused his cheeks. His eyes drew forth from the funk they were in and stayed there, all shadow gone from them now.

I returned from the kitchen with two beers and sat across the glass table from her. Her legs were crossed, demure. She took a pull off the beer and seemed to prepare herself.

"Can you believe it?" she began. "I'm a reporter working on a story. My leads turned up something here that, I think, might show the origin of what I'm after and, actually, be the end of my chase."

"A reporter." I was intrigued. I tried to keep from sounding condescending when I asked, "In Norwich? What could ever happen here that's worth reporting?"

"You would be surprised." came the enigmatic reply. I decided to change the subject.

"Why don't I show you your room?"

Claura was glad he changed the subject. You can't risk spooking him too soon.

They took their beers towards the stairwell when the door opposite opened, and an older man emerged. The smile that came suddenly to his stern features was genuine.

"Hello," he said.

"Claura," Jack said, directing a hand to indicate the newcomer,

"Allow me to introduce my father, Jack Senior. Pop, Ms. Roberts, here, is looking to rent a room."

"Well," Jack Sr. began, "They do get prettier every season." He turned a wise man's eye to his son before turning back to Claura. He took her hand in a mature handshake, nonetheless.

"I'm delighted to meet you, Claura. Please make yourself at home."

"You let me know if he gets out of line," he jerked a thumb over his shoulder at his boy. "I'd be happy to take his place."

"POP! Really?"

I was mortified, but Claura was laughing right along with my father.

To see two war horses giggling like school children would have amazed anybody. If they knew Pop the way I did, they'd think he was hitting the bottle. I knew he was totally dry, though.

Naw. He didn't fool me for a minute. Any minute he'll be reciting the 'rules of the house' before getting down to the bill of rights. Right?

Claura laughed harder than she had in years. She was actually glad she came here. "You darling man." And then leaned in to plant a peck on one grizzled cheek.

"Be sure I will, Ms. Roberts. I'm sure there are a few old tricks Jack's never seen."

Finishing their laugh at Jack's expense, she started up the stairs after him. Her hand slid up the ancient banister.

She pretended she didn't see his father enjoying the rearview.

"I'm so sorry," Jack was saying. "He's normally not like this."

"Oh, he's sweet," Claura said with a rare warmth. Rare for her. They continued, stairs creaking up to the third floor.

"Who, Pop? The man that put the fear of God into me as a child? You really haven't met him."

"Well, here it is." Jack opened a door at the end of the hall. "It's really not much."

Claura peeked past him in the living room.

"Wow, are you kidding? Does every room have a den?"

"Yes. Each room has a parlor and a small kitchenette we added. This one only has a single bedroom. The ones on the second floor have two."

She looked around at the decor. The apartment was well accoutered to fit a style from a bygone era. Handmade furniture of carved wood and filigree cushions matched the dated wallpaper's felt accents.

She felt like she'd stepped back in time. The shelves were filled with porcelain statuary and plastic flowers. She couldn't help running a finger for dust.

"You're alone, here, though. There's no one else on the third floor, so you don't even have to share the bathroom."

Claura was inspecting the surroundings, but, inside she was amazed at the tastefulness of it all. Jack noticed her scrutinizing closely.

"We have someone clean and dust regularly. The cushions have even been replaced to fit the period. You can't imagine how hard it was to find the wallpaper. This house is over two hundred and thirty years old."

"It's amazing!" Claura breathed. "However, did you find all of this art?"

"Oh, it's original from the times. This house has always been in my family. Five generations."

"it would be a shame if it didn't see six."

Now, there she goes again, Claura thought. She guessed her biological clock had to start ticking sometime.

It was sweet of Jack not to take notice of her intentions. She hadn't intended to butter these guys up just to get as much information as she could out of them.

This was just happening naturally. It was the fact that there had never been room in her life for such dalliance, before, that felt so alien. She decided she wasn't going to let it stop.

"Can I help with your things?" Jack was saying. He had caught her off guard.

"Hmm?" she turned, her last thoughts interrupted.

"Your stuff." Jack clarified. "Can I help you bring them up?"

"Sweet. Just like your father."

She was making me blush again. I could feel the fullness in my cheeks. She had to be messing with me.

As we reached the second-floor landing, we ran into little Lucy, holding her kitten. She was looking up at the tough girl descending behind me. The feelings of awe stretched her mouth open.

"Hello, Lucy," I said. "This is Claura. She's gonna be staying with us a while."

"It's a pleasure to meet you, Lucy." she was saying. She took a knee, bringing her gruff self-down to the girl's level with ladylike ease. "And who might this be?"

"This is Mr. Jingaling. We call him Jingles for short." Then she asked with a child's innocence: "Are you a superhero?"

"Well," Claura said, standing back up. "I have been a soldier. I like to think some of us turned out to be heroes in the end."

Evidently, the bright day wasn't confined to indoors. The sun greeted us as we stepped down from the porch and through the trees. Fallen leaves rustled in in the breeze. Their faint aroma smelled of sandalwood, rising through the skeletal tree branches towards the cloudless sky.

Claura's SUV was parked on the curb. She, first, slung a large green duffel over her back by its straps and reached in to drag out a large black box.

No. As a cloud finally made itself known, covering the sun, I noticed it was a chest. A chill had nothing to do with the autumn wind galvanized my spine. This was a black plastic travel chest. Still, I had a grim sense of foreboding as I looked at it.

I wasn't thinking about an old, dusty chest in a cobweb-filled attic. At least, I don't think I was conscious.

Claura was enjoying the look of bewilderment on Jack's face at the sight of her duffel bag. She slung it on like a giant, green, sausage-shaped backpack. As she dragged that end of her gorilla chest to the edge of the tailgate, she could actually feel the chills running down his spine.

She looked at his eyes. They held a faraway look, and the shadows in his eye sockets had returned. The cloud passed from over the sun and, just like that, the moment had passed, as well. All was bright and sunny as he grabbed the opposite end she was angling in his direction.

He helped with his end without hesitation. Claura wondered if he had registered his feeling, consciously, himself or not. From over his shoulder, she couldn't tell as he led her by the plastic footlocker.

It was easy going all the way up to the third-floor room, of which she was now the occupant.

"Well," Jack huffed as they recrossed the threshold. "If there's ever anything you need, don't hesitate."

"Do you stay with your father?"

"No!" I said a bit too loudly.

"I'm on the second floor, across from the Hartleys. The laundry room is right there. If you'd like me to show you."

Then she stopped me by placing a hand on my arm.

"Look," she said. "Why don't I just save you the agony and suggest you take me out to dinner tonight. I'm sure you know something nearby that serves the local cuisine. I need to get freshened up, but, say about 7:30?"

Did she just ask me out?

I struggled to keep smooth and not stutter.

"Well, make me an offer I can't refuse!"

Nice.

She gave my arm a reassuring squeeze and let go hopefully before she could feel the hammering of my heart.

"I'll just meet you downstairs. 7:30." I said with the bare minimum of head nods and slipped out the door.

I had to stop on the first landing to catch my breath.

Claura stood with her back against the door. Classic love-struck pose, she thought. I'm finally losing it!

After all this time, the nightmares, the horror. This is what it takes to drive me out of my mind.

2. Dinner and a Movie Role

Norwich has no shortage of restaurants within walking distance. Mostly fast food. I thought Claura deserved better, and she was looking for a good time, so to speak. Or maybe just to hang out and have a beer.

I figured a taste of the local nightlife couldn't hurt, and the Old Tymes was a bar and grill with a real family atmosphere. The jukebox was always on. There was even room for couples to dance. It would be the perfect place to unwind and, maybe, find out more about her.

She filled his thoughts with nothing but questions.

What was she doing here? She said she was chasing something.

91

What was she really like? What kind of past did it take to shape a person like Claura Roberts?

He hoped he liked the answers.

Jack was waiting for her at the bottom of the steps when Claura came down. Despite the tight jeans and loose-fitting top, she felt like she was winding down the staircase like a girl headed to her prom.

She had never gone to prom. What did she know?

All resentment of her past felt washed away, though, since her arrival to this fairy tale place called Norwich. Or maybe, it was the house. She felt like she had come home. The added luxury of a fully furnished apartment freed her from obligations to obtain more belongings while providing for her needs. She couldn't have wished for more.

And now, she found herself going out on a date! It must have been, like, decades since she last tried. She couldn't even recall a name, a face, nor the place. What country was she in back then?

She gave up the train of thought as she looked down on her new friend. Jack had cleaned up nice. The red flannel really suited him. His hair was still doing its own thing but managed to conform to a style. His brusque face now had the expression of a schoolboy looking up at his prom date.

There was a look of hunger he couldn't hide, but, on him, it was like a compliment.

True to form, there was his Dad. He stepped out of his parlor just as she reached the bottom.

"Well…" he said leeringly. "You kids going out?"

"Yeah," Jack replied, caught out. "Claura wanted to sample some of the local atmospheres."

"That's just fine." He looked longingly at Claura. "You look lovely," he said as if she were wearing an evening gown instead of blue jeans and Docs.

"You kids have a good time." Then he turned to waggle a finger at her.

"Now you be careful with him, honey. Don't go breaking his heart. It doesn't have that much mileage on it."

"Thanks, Mr. Lawrence. It's good to know I won't have to compete with any memories."

"No worries there," Jack muttered. "They would never stand a chance."

She gave Jack Sr.'s arm a polite squeeze then hooked her arm under Jack's. With smiles all around, the couple stepped out.

The place was pretty packed, but we'd gotten a table and were getting acquainted over burgers.

"Cryptozoology is a relatively acceptable branch of science, now." Claura was saying. "Aside from the usual skepticism, there's a legitimacy to the work I'd always struggled to find in all my prior jobs."

"The Times isn't just your basic Walmart tabloid. They only state the facts as they're backed up in the lab reports. I also provide interesting enough photos to fill out the magazine's pages. Once in a while, they give me the cover."

"How much do you like the travel?" I asked.

"Oh, it has some perks. I meet a lot of interesting people and get to leave before they can get attached."

Was that concern on his face? Claura wondered. He must not think he's all that—one of my favorite traits on a man.

Just then, as if to prove the point, out slunk the self-proclaimed alpha male, walking up behind Jack and out of his past.

The look of smug superiority dripping off his unshaven face was as obvious as the three cronies looking on from one of the higher tables.

"Hiya, Jacky," he bawled, slapping one big hand on his shoulder. "Where have YOU been lately?" Then ogled Claura shamelessly.

"Where SHE'S been my whole life?" He not only answered himself but laughed at his own jokes.

"Oh, hey Ray. You know it's Jack. Not Jacky."

"Come to ruin another perfectly good evening, I see."

"You know it."

Jack leaned over the table apologetically. "Ray Donovan has been stealing my dates since the fourth grade."

"Don't you ever get tired of yourself?" Jack aimed over his shoulder. "All those ladies sure seemed to pretty quick."

"Naw," he brayed, sincerely not taking the hint. "I never get tired of whatchoo want. I figured I'd go for the record."

"Whadyoo say, sweetheart?" Did he really get this act to work for him at his age? Claura thought. She began digging in her purse.

"One second. I think I've got it right here."

Oh. I thought. Is she looking for a pen to write her number down? I realized I didn't have it yet.

Things didn't look good as Ray leaned over to get a better view at what she was doing or just down her blouse.

"I thought I had one." She said.

"What's that?" Ray rudely asked.

"Well," Claura said. "Since you came all the way over here to measure your dick, I thought I'd better have a magnifying glass!" She graced him with an icy grin.

"Hah!" I couldn't stop the laugh if you paid me. Stifling it with effort into evil snickers, Claura joined me in, chuckling as everyone nearby, who couldn't help but hear the exchange, applauded her.

What a woman, I thought.

Ray slipped away like a smacked puppy, real fast. His head was really low. Jack hoped that would be the last they saw of him.

"Well." Claura was looking at him. "Does a girl have to suggest you take me on the dance floor, now, too?"

The evening wound down after a few beers and dancing to five songs. Some of them slow. Jack was keeping count.

It had been a perfect night out, and they were crossing the parking lot. Ray, with his buddies, wasn't going to let it stand so easily.

Before they knew it, Jack found his arms hemmed by two while another laid a fist up his gut.

Ray, foolishly, tried to pin Claura against the side of someone's truck.

"Did you think you were gonna make a fool of me so easily?" He husked in her face. The yeast on his breath would have made a lesser woman gag.

Keeping eye contact with the prick, she was really reaching, again, into her purse.

The other three continued to lay into Jack, not really doing much harm.

A sharp report split the night. The gunshot lit up their little party. The flash of light bounced quickly off the vehicles around them.

The top of Ray's left boot squirted blood like a Monty Python skit. His ass hit the ground as he cried out, trying to cradle it.

Claura had pulled a colt 45, the same caliber of the bullet that punched a neat hole through the top of Ray's boot.

As Jack regained his night vision, he watched as she held the smoking barrel to Ray's head, now. His buddies held their hands up in surrender.

"Quit yer whinin'," she threatened. "I was aiming for your dick. Guess that size is good for something after all."

Jack saw the beast in her eyes for the first time. Aimed away from him as it was, she still made him shudder. He dusted himself off as she aimed the pistol at the other three in turn.

"You Cocksuckers got something to say?!"

She put the gun against Ray's head again, holding them with her gaze.

"I'm in my right to shoot this fucker dead in self-defense. You all would have been complicit in third-degree rape, not to mention assault and battery on my boyfriend, there."

Did she just call me her boyfriend?

"Now get the FUCK OUT of HERE and tell your Mommas their lookin' for you!"

Once again, she brought applause from the gathered crowd, who were keeping a distance to be sure. But the ruckus had brought curious onlookers from the restaurant.

The would-be attackers stumbled off, not one shout of "Crazy Bitch!" escaping.

They were too afraid.

Claura faced me, alone. In the dark, our faces were inches apart. I panted with adrenaline. She hardly breathed. The gun was put up, and the crowd had gone back inside.

I had no idea what to say. Was I aroused or shit-scared? I didn't question her sanity. She had a different look on her face now.

It wasn't sorrow. She wasn't looking for forgiveness, but the need was there. Then, all at once, it was unmistakable.

She pressed her mouth against mine with a ferocity that pinned me against the opposite truck.

What a woman.

3. The Morning After

I had expected to walk her to her door like she had asked, and that would have been it. Instead, she grabbed me gently by the wrist and led me inside like she didn't want me to bolt on her.

Not likely. I might not have been around the block as much as she had, but my awe of her was in danger of becoming outright worshipping devotion. I'd follow her into Hell and tweak Satan's nipples. All she had to do was ask.

Our lovemaking was inexpert. I figured she would have had more experience, but she was obviously making up for a lost time, same as I. Still, we had fun and laughed as we moaned. In the end, she fell asleep in my arms, holding tight like she didn't dare let go.

I drifted off, wondering again at the dichotomy of this girl curled up with one cheek on my chest. Her body seemed more scarred than her psyche. Tattoos adorned.

She was rough against my baby soft, unworn skin. Lack of exercise provided her with an ideal pillow. I didn't want to let go, either.

When morning came, nevertheless, the sunlight found me alone in her bed. I had an instant to register a fear that it was all a dream. She couldn't be real.

Then my eyes focused on the cup of coffee she thrust towards my face. She giggled at the sight. Eyes crossed through the steam; I grasped it in both hands like a starving raccoon.

I was still exhausted, yet she looked fresh as a punk rock daisy wearing my shirt. She kissed me quickly before favoring me with the view of her long legs flowing from its hem as she walked away. She sat on a settee where she had set her laptop.

She must have been up for hours. She was vocal last night but now was working quietly, allowing me all the time I needed to rouse myself and join her.

I was about to find out what it was that drew her attention to this place, what it was that brought her into my life.

I looked down once I reached her side. What I saw on the laptop brought up that feeling of foreboding once again.

She was looking at a house three doors down from this very doorstep.

"That's the Mackenzie House," I noted.

"I know," Claura said with reverence. "That's also the beginning of my trail."

"It's been on permanent open house since the last owners," I added. "Noone will live there for very long, but nobody knows why." The feelings of foreboding began to morph into a childhood memory. It wasn't a good one.

"What are you investigating, and what does it have to do with that house?" Why did I feel as soon as I asked those questions like, somehow, I already had the answers?

"Get dressed." was her reply. "I want to show you something."

Claura waited patiently while he got ready. She had already been to the MacKenzie House once that morning, confirming what she already knew she'd find. She had said she would return with her fiancé, inwardly enjoying the deception on so many levels.

She didn't need the validation. She had known, all along, she wasn't crazy. This time, she truly needed help for the first time. Fate had thrown this man in her lap for better or worse. *snicker* She had to handle him with extra special care. She knew. The truth was going to traumatize him.

She wasn't aware, yet, the extent of his involvement.

They walked hand in hand down the sidewalk. It was over in moments, moments Jack felt the need to savor. Something told him things weren't going to be the same. *Too soon*, he thought. *I don't want the good time to stop.*

Claura led him up the steps and through the front door. Letting his hand go, she allowed Jack to take in his surroundings.

The home was dated much like his own. It was just smaller. The place echoed ominously. It was still and bare, wall to wall, except for a few lamps and wall hangings. Not for the first time, he tried to recall what had happened here.

"Claura?" He called out to her, searching. He found her in the living room, pressing the side of her face to the mirror that had been left on the wall.

"What are you doing?" He watched her in bewilderment. She was looking into the mirror at such an extreme angle her eyes were almost looking down the wall.

"There used to be a grandfather clock in the hall." Claura was saying.

"What?" I asked. "How could you know that?" I suddenly got the feeling there truly was something otherworldly about her. *Was she psychic?*

"Oh, I can see it. I'm looking at it right now."

"That's crazy!" I didn't mean to say it like that. It just came out. I know I didn't mean anything by it. Fortunately, she did, too.

"You think so?" She was smiling impishly. "Have a look for yourself!" Her smile became triumphant as I placed my cheek where she had hers on the mirror.

At first, I wasn't looking at it right. All I saw was the empty hall. Then, out of the corner of my eye, it was there—just an edge of it at the last possible verge of being out of sight in the mirror.

It was the corner of a grandfather clock.

I switched back and forth from looking outwards at the hall then back to the mirror a few times. I tried to gauge what point in the hall I was viewing in the mirror.

"You see it?" Her voice got a little shrill. She clapped her hands together and cackled like a mad scientist. "I knew it! I knew this was the place." She was starting to frighten me again. She saw that and visibly toned back down.

Suddenly, she was the professional. She was the reporter sharing her findings, though she did it with a trace of melodrama.

"I've come across this twice before. All of them are sites of mysterious disappearances. They might not have been acknowledged at the time. Hell, some were actually covered up for years! But this time, he was sloppy."

"Whoa," I said, one hand held out. "Did you say 'He'?"

Claura's look of concern struck me. She was trying hard not to scare me. "Come on. Let's get out of here, and I'll explain. You need to hear the whole story."

I didn't know what she wanted to tell me, but I was sure glad to get out of that place.

4. The Whole Story

They were back in Claura's room. She pulled him to her, wrapping him in her arms, and began kissing him. He relaxed in her arms, and she paused, looking deeply into his eyes, searching.

She gauged him carefully. She didn't want to seem like she was playing him. He could be lost to her any moment. She had to help him be strong. Stronger than he'd ever been before.

She needed him in more ways than one.

She sat me down in front of the laptop and brought up a map. It was of the entire United States with hundreds of red dots stretching from Connecticut to Arizona. They made a meandering trail. He saw the one furthest east was, what must have been, three doors down.

The Mackenzie House.

She reached over me, and I watched her strong hand enter something on the keyboard. She had changed the dot next door from red to green.

"These are all disappearances?" I asked.

"Yes," she said, simply. She sat down beside me and held my hand.

"When did these happen? How long did it go on?"

"These are only the ones I have been able to confirm. They range back, some, twenty-five years. From all indications, it's still going on."

"Where?" I was starting to get heated. "Arizona?!"

She was starting to get worried. I guess she was afraid of what I'd say. This all went from reporting to real way too fast. My head was spinning.

She got up and walked to her kitchenette. My eyes followed her the whole way, thankfully, distracted by her beauty.

I heard the refrigerator door and tinkling glass.

"You need a beer." She had returned with two bottles. Neither of us cared what time it was.

Claura watched him down half the bottle right off. After a moment, she began again.

"You've got to understand. What caused the disappearances has been around a long time. It predates human history."

"Things like this have plagued mankind throughout the millennia. As long as there have been people, there have been *things that go bump in the night*; you know what I'm talking about?"

"You've heard tales of nocturnal visitations." On her laptop, she brought up the familiar images of the Fuselli paintings. White women draped over their beds: Dark, ape-like beings crouched on their chests.

"In every country, in each century, there are constant accounts. Sufferers from sleep paralysis reported seeing an old hag. The people near bodies of water had Jenny Greenteeth and Nelly Longarms."

"Baba-Yaga in Russia. Cucuy in Mexico. The Boogeyman. Arabian Ghuls. As far back as the earliest civilizations."

"For all we know, it's one creature."

I had to know.

"So, explain the grandfather clock. What was I seeing?" I asked.

She took a pull off her beer before answering.

"This thing comes from another dimension, entirely. I shit you not. It is coming out of the mirrors."

"It actually gets around by moving behind, what we know of as reality. Like a ghost, it walks through walls. It can move from one place to another, unseen. The same distance it takes to move from house to house, it does so outside our space of four dimensions through its opposite, equal distance six or eight dimensions deep."

"That's impossible." I breathed, but I wasn't convincing myself too well.

"I don't know how, but it manages to hollow a space that corresponds with the angles our eyes see through reflective surfaces. Any reflective surface."

"So, explain the grandfather clock."

She clapped her hands together. Holding her hands intertwined, she pointed with both index fingers.

"You see, he doesn't just make people disappear. He kills them. Every last one. Drinks their blood and mutilated their bodies. I think it likes to eat flesh, but its main food source is blood. The blood of little children."

"So, you can imagine the mess that would have to make. It would be discovered if it painted the whole room with the blood of its victims. It can't leave a trace. So, it found a way."

"To keep his crime scenes clean, it simply drags them through a mirror then out of sight from this side. It can butcher them without leaving a drop of blood. I think it even gets off on torturing some like it can feed off fear."

"As for the clock, I'm willing to bet all the belongings in that house were shoved out of sight. Their reflections, anyway. Here, on this side, they probably just ceased to exist!"

"Whole families have disappeared from homes, apartment complexes, even hotel rooms. Then it moves their stuff aside and, POOF! the place is empty like the owners just packed up and left."

I could only shake my head, trying to wrap it around all this.

"Have you seen this thing?" I asked.

"Oh, much more than that. But I'll find a way to stop it." She got up and shook a fist at the ceiling.

"You got that, Blood Banshee?! I'll get you, YOU BASTARD!"

"Wait, wait." I put an arm out to bar her.

"What did you just say?!"

Claura could see she'd struck the right nerve. She just didn't know which yet.

Jack dove at the laptop, quickly pulling up a page. Claura angled behind him, looking over his shoulder as he typed furiously.

"Gayle House?" she asked, totally thrown. "Where on Earth is that?"

"Nowhere!" Jack exclaimed. "At least, nowhere real. Look and tell me what you think!"

She looked at the picture of an old mail-order ad. The thing in the corner next to the dilapidated house made her jump back three feet.

"Hoah!" Claura yawped, one hand flung over her mouth in horror.

"Holy SHIT!" She was getting frantic, now, too.

"Where in Hell did you find THAT?!"

"COMIC BOOKS!" I howled!

"It's an ad for an old scare record from the seventies! I guess it really WAS haunted!"

"That's IT! That's IT!" Claura was shrieking. "How did you know?"

"You said 'Blood Banshee.' Well, that's what it's called on the record. There's no other mention of that name anywhere."

I scratched my head. "Well, maybe that other haunted house record, but nowhere in legends or fantasy novels. Dungeons and Dragons. NOTHING!"

Then it hit me. I took her by the wrist, this time.

"You've gotta come with me," I said. She was visibly shaking. I half dragged her as we plunged down the stairs and into the back sitting room.

I went straight to the stereo and began ransacking the vinyl collection.

"It's gotta be here." I was muttering.

What did I do with it back then? Did I put it away? All the comics and junk from that old chest were sold long ago. I made a tidy living off it for years.

But the record, I never saw again after that night.

Kneeling back, I thought how the room hadn't changed in over twenty years.

I remembered taking the disc off the turntable once the shock had worn off. The boogeyman had come and gone. I put it on top of the stereo's lid.

I looked at its clear form covering the still turntable with its stylus arm at rest.

Then it hit me. The stereo had never been moved! I looked behind it, and sure enough, there it was. Against the wall, on the floor, covered in speaker wires and dust.

The Gayle House Haunting.

Claura stood behind me as I held it up like a winning prize, then out like a venomous snake.

I turned to look at her. The horror was dawning on me as I looked past her at the sliding glass door. Further back in my mind's eye, I realized Claura's reaction was correct. If she really had seen it, she'd know how accurate the picture ad was.

I was in shock. Transported back to that night, I was thirteen again. I raised a trembling hand and pointed at the door.

"I saw it there. First, it was in the reflection behind me. Then, when I played the record, it was in the window, deep in the corner of the room!"

"Then it moved that way." My finger followed my gaze as it moved to the right. "Then it was gone."

The hand went over my mouth in dawning horror. Oh. My. GOD!!!

"The Mackenzies…" as tears started to fall, Claura was there holding me, making shushing sounds.

I looked up. Our eyes met. We were both in tears, streaming down our cheeks with guilt.

"I'm responsible. The Mackenzies. The disappearances, Everybody! I set it loose!!!"

"I know, I know…" Claura was blubbering, having nothing else to say.

"They are all dead because of me."

"You couldn't have known. You were just a kid!"

"Yeah. But that doesn't change the fact. I have a reason to be horrified, be guilty."

We were kneeling in front of each other, wiping at our tears. Claura took a deep sigh and rolled up her left shirt sleeve.

Exposing the nasty scars that wrung her forearm, she looked deep into my eyes.

"I can do you one better."

Then she told me about her junior year in high school.

Venice, Italy
The Vatican Archives
Papal Paramilitary Division
LEVEL 1

The page rushed into his supervisor's office. Coming to a halt, he straightened his three-piece suit and the stack of files in his hands.

"Cardinal Commander!" he blurted. "We've had a breach!"

A white-haired man in regal attire spun in his command throne to face his agitated subordinate.

"How? What level?"

"Level Twelve. Sector Thirteen."

The look of horror on the Cardinal's face was not exaggerated.

"The Forbidden Texts Library?"

"Yes, eminence." He held forward the pile of records in his hands.

"Show me!" he barked, spinning back around in his command pulpit. He rose to his feet, stood before the lectern, and looked out over the rows of technicians.

Sunken in the pit', his menials worked over their computer terminals in endless surveillance of the outside world.

This underground citadel had been the secret heart of the Vatican for centuries. Never before had there been a cause to view security footage from within the secret archives.

From here, in the command center, spiritual threats and supernatural events were monitored—the many levels beneath housed artifacts and documents from the dawn of time. More religious objects, art, and accounts adorned its vaults than any conspiracy theorist could possibly imagine.

Each level was a square mile layer of glass and concrete halls spreading outwards from the central lift. Ventilation extended in an array of ductwork from the central shaft. It was possible to see through the glass walls from one end to the other given enough light. Security cameras and multiple sensor arrays were suspended in overlapping intervals; their red and green LED's filled the air with a faux Christmas atmosphere.

Optical, laser, audio, sonar, radar, and temperature variance were always on the alert—even olfactory. Nothing was left to chance, and there were no blind corners and, around the clock, human operators ensured there could be no hacking of their feeds in their endless shifts. An entire division of their army was devoted to the secrecy and security of sacred materials.

There had never been a breach.

"Do we have any footage?" The Cardinal was getting impatient.

"Yes, eminence." A three-second piece of footage flickered on the main screen in the distance fifty meters tall.

"Report!" The old man shouted. "Is this all we have?!"

The page was quaking in terror. His voice broke as he began his report, swallowing convulsively.

"At 2349, motion detectors registered a brief spike in Sector Thirteen that lasted half a second. Fifteen minutes later, thermal sensors detected a rise of twenty-nine point three degrees near one of the briefing lecterns down hall 48."

"No one was recorded entering or leaving either area, and the lift was not operated. The lift hasn't been accessed in twelve years."

"A security team was dispatched to both locations and immediately dusted the area for prints. They were given orders to touch nothing and secure the areas."

"Very good." The Cardinal found he was temporarily modified by the succinctness of the report.

"What was discovered?"

The page opened a file folder to read.

"The Librarium that had been accessed proved to be missing one tome from its shelves. It was, subsequently found in the lecture hall, Hall 48."

"The room also housed a number of blessed objects, objects of martial intent."

"Weapons?" the Cardinal turned to the page to inquire.

"Yes, your eminence. The room collected various documents and accouterments for combating a specific enemy."

"Well…that enemy being?"

"Ghouls, your holiness."

"Ugh." the commander grunted. "Filthy things. There hasn't been an outbreak of their sort since, what was it, 1320?"

"1325." chimed the page. "The missing weapons proved to be staked, holiness. Three of them."

"The Stakes?" the Cardinal asked with reticence.

"Yes, eminence. Three from the collection of stakes carved from the Cross. The very Cross of the Crucifixion, itself."

"Blasphemous…" his commander muttered.

"If I may, your holiness." He picked up the Cardinal's remote. "On the lectern was the missing tome. The German manuscript 'Das Buch Der Ghuls.'

It was opened to these pages." He clicked the remote to change the view screen to project the image of the open book.

The Cardinal recoiled involuntarily.

"The Blood Banshee..." he whispered. He needed a moment before asking: "Was there anything else?"

"Yes, your lordship. A scrap of paper with a scribbled address, a picture postcard, and the half-eaten remains of an American confectionary. An 'Oh Henry' bar."

"DNA analysis of the last bite yielded no match in the worldwide database. Neither did the fingerprints. The postcard is of a tourist site in the American state of Arizona. It's a science center. The picture is from its main attraction, a Mirror maze. It's quite a striking photo."

The Cardinal was not impressed.

"And the address?" He asked.

"101 North Main Street. Norwich, Connecticut. The United States of America."

5. Research and Developments

Jack and Claura were at his computer, now. The tube monitor was a bit out of date, and the tower supported a layer of dust, but the hard drive still got Skype.

As the screen warmed up, Jack was already typing. He opened a live chat with an old acquaintance.

"Kurt Dameroux," he told Claura, "is the guy I sold all the novelties to from the trunk." Jack adjusted the webcam.

"He's a collector and a historian. He has actually published a number of books. I've read the one he wrote about the history of the Johnson Smith Novelty Company."

"It was great. He showcased each ad with the promise of the items alongside the quality of the things that were delivered."

"Most of the mail-order ads and merchandise were from them. It certainly fits the time period. If anyone knows about the Gayle House, it'll be Kurt."

We were in luck. He was there to take The call. The screen came alive with the close-up view of Kurt in his menagerie.

A bearded man, in the latter years of his 30's, like us, adjusted himself into view as he settled into his office chair.

Shelves of joy buzzers and other vintage novelties spilled from in front of the wide array of reproduction Topstone masks in the background. Their latex countenances lined every available space in view.

In a specially sealed glass display case prominently set directly over his shoulder was an actual Verne Langdon Zombie. Its lumpy green face and slitted eyes stared blankly at us from under its blonde surfer hairdo.

It was his prized possession. He even set the certificate of authenticity in there with it.

Kurt adjusted his glasses on the screen. The tiny window in the corner held the image of myself, with Claura peeking over my shoulder.

"Jack! Great to see you. It's been a long time. You've got something for me today?"

"Hello," he continued in his best Lando Calrisian. "What have we here?" He had seen Claura.

"Dude. Please tell me it's her." Now he really sounded like a big kid. He recovered quickly.

"No. Seriously, how do you do, Miss?"

"Claura Roberts," I said. "I'd like you to meet Kurt Dameroux, vintage historian extraordinaire."

"Hello." She waved.

"Clearly, the pleasure is all his," Kurt complained jokingly. "No. Really, it's nice to meet you."

"So, what can I do for you, buddy?"

I drove right into it. There was no time to waste.

"We need all the information you have on that old haunted house scare record. Y'know, the Gayle House Haunting."

"Oh." He entered something on his keyboard. "You mean this thing?"

Our screen was filled with the same ad we had looked at earlier.

"That's the one," I said.

"I was just going over it myself." He said. "It's got an entry on YouTube, now. I even downloaded a recording of it."

The distinctive, moose call howl came over my speakers as he played it. Claura stifled her gasp with one hand.

"Pretty awful, isn't it?"

"You have no idea." I was bemoaning.

"Hmmm?" Said Kurt. His face was back.

106

It was my turn to recover.

"I said, do you have any idea who might have done the recording? Where it might have been done?"

"Well. As you can see in the ad, the only address for ordering is a post office box in Flushing, New York. But I think I might have tracked down a recording studio that was active back then."

"You see, it was the first of its kind. Then good ol' Johnson Smith Company put one out and set the standard for all the others that came out for years after."

"But the Gayle House, whatever that was, had to be a true one-off. There was only a small group of recording technicians with the proper equipment back then."

"Studying the voices from popular radio shows I was able to find, I think I may have narrowed it down."

"It WAS affiliated with Johnson Smith. A guy named Jean Shepherd was a big-time recording artist and radio personality. The stories told about his antics made him out to be a real hellraiser."

Claura and I exchanged looks. "What do you mean?" she asked.

"Well," Kurt continued. "Legend has it; he made a big influence on the radio advertising of that era. A couple of things he reported to listeners to look out for didn't even exist. There was such a demand that artists had to, then, come up with the stuff. That was very edgy for those times."

"Nowadays, they call it fraud," I noted.

"Nonsense. He was an innovator, if not an outright inventor, himself."

"Anyway, he passed away in 1999, but the sound effects man I was able to track down. One, Bruce Horowitz by name. He's still alive. He dropped out of recording right after he did The Haunting. Some kind of nervous breakdown."

"You can find him in a retirement home on the easternmost part of New York state. 'On the beautiful shores of Lake Erie.'" he said in a radio announcer's false tones. "It's called Saint Columbans."

"Anyway, that's all I've got. Anyone else involved was either a nobody or didn't want to risk being attached to it."

"Thanks, Kurt," I said. "That's great work. I bet they didn't even keep records for stuff like this back then."

"I know, right? Not like it is now, huh?"

"You really did your homework. But I've gotta ask," I thought the timing was too good to be a coincidence. "What made you look?"

He dug down by his side. Then he pulled up a new mask.

"What do you think of this?" He asked.

He was holding up a scaly-looking blue latex monster mask. The yellow eyes and enormous fangs were unmistakable from beneath a black, burlap hood.

Claura had to look away. She covered it well with an "Eeeeew!"

"Pretty ugly, huh? It's from the 'Devil's Workshop' I'd say it's pretty accurate. Don't you think?"

"Just like the real thing." I heard Claura mutter. He got that quizzical look again. Before he could say anything else, I signed out.

"Thanks again, buddy!" Then he and that face were gone from the screen and not too soon.

Claura was looking at her cellphone. She held a page from Google Maps towards me.

"Saint Columbans on the Lake. It's right by the 90. If we leave now, we can get there this evening."

She was getting that determined look. I was about to see her in action once again.

Vatican Archives
Level 13
Hall 48

The glass walls of the scriptorium reflected the image of the grim gathering back at its occupants in the dim lighting. They looked like a gathering because that's what this was.

Father Confessor Magnus Opussino had no illusions about that. It was just another mission brief to him. The location might have been unusual had he been in any other line of work. Mission briefs were handled on Level One. This level housed ancient artifacts. Whatever was being disseminated here today must involve material directly from here that was restricted to this section.

Satisfied with his assessment, he sat quietly behind his team waiting, patiently to be 'illuminated.'

The pun was not lost on him. Inwardly, he afforded himself a wry smile that never surfaced onto his patrician features. He was always the picture of discipline. The Papacy was aware of his imagination and wit. That was why he was the team leader. Most of his team might have been more uncivilized or less thoughtful, but that was the nature of their purpose. He only required two immediate subordinates with which he could corroborate or delegate. The other four were better as mindless brutes.

The team of Excoriators was raised from birth in the martial tenets of the church. Bred from the longest line of the finest Christian crusaders, they grew into their positions as they were trained from their infancy.

Those that survived the training of their youth went on to serve the church as a secret paramilitary group. Steeped in the mysteries of the spiritual, they confronted threats in realms most physical. Moral threats were, undeniably, violent where demonology was concerned. Their weapons were carnal by definition.

While Father Magnus wasn't musing on these subjects, they were a given; he was interested in the fact that the Cardinal Commander, himself, was in attendance to this brief.

That was odd, too. What was most striking was the presence of two savants. The heretics automatically struck a nerve with him, but it was not his place to question. He preferred the methods he had trained in, the extensive technology of the day, and his own wits. What were they doing here? And where was their third?

They were known to stay together in their seclusion. A representative of a culture that predated the founding of Christianity, the magi were throwbacks from the most primitive doctrines of religious belief and power. Their methods had not changed from the time of the Stone Age. The augury of animal intestines and casting of lots was not unheard of with their type. Forbidden practices were their forte. They were only tolerated as long as they remained devoted to God and the church.

Personally, Magnus had no use for their gifts. He could always count on his conscience and training to complete his mission satisfactorily. He didn't need to be told the Will of God. Certainly, not by some unbaptized heathen.

Magnus had waited long enough. The priest at the lectern, obviously, had no clue how to start this briefing.

109

Newbie, he spurned to himself. He rose with military poise. Boots apart, hands crossed behind his back.

"Cardinal Commander, what is the reason for this briefing? Are we ready to get on with it?"

In response, the elderly pontificate got to his feet and replaced the sweating priest at the briefing lectern. He placed a consoling hand on his shoulder and indicated him to a seat.

"I understand your impatience, Commander. Team Aleph is not called for the lightest of matters, though. With the passage of recent events, you must forgive Father Oleander his reticence. He has been through quite an ordeal."

"What do you mean?" Father Clovis, one of Magnus's seconds, inquired from his seat. "What has happened?"

"I can only say that in the preliminary survey of the facts gathered for this briefing, we lost one of the savants, and Father Dorian, as you can see, is no longer here to brief you."

"While in the midst of scrying part of the evidence, the savant became enraged. He attacked Father Dorian, who was standing too close before we could stop him."

"He then died, the autopsy proved, from a brain aneurism."

"Father Dorian's throat was severely damaged when the savant tried to remove it with his teeth. He remains in critical condition."

The Cardinal looked down to the lectern a moment, struggling for words. He saw that it was left to him. He would have to complete this briefing himself.

"I can begin by informing you of a security breach. A breach of this very hall." He paused to let that sink in. The look of shock on the team of exorcists was immediate and audible.

Even Fathers Sax and Corelli were able to grasp the magnitude of that statement, and they were not recruited for their intelligence. At the moment, their bulky frames shuddered. Every team member's eyes were wide and very much attentive, now.

"Yes. A breach. The lift was not accessed, nor the air ducts. I can see you are aware of the impossibility of such a feat, as it were. Minimal sensor returns and a few seconds of footage were all the telemetry had to offer. The alarms weren't even tripped."

"Was there any sign of a hack?" Magnus leapt for the first conclusion that came to mind.

"No. All systems were functioning normally. The software was not under threat. Whoever did this or how it happened remains a mystery."

"Spiritual, then." Magnus was not one to let things go. "Is it possible the intruder was not physical?"

"A good supposition, but again, no. The intruder was, by all evidence, a normal human."

"As you all know, supernatural entities can radiate any level of cold. Demons can manifest with extreme heat or with traces of sulfur. This interloper registered, briefly, at 99.3 degrees. He's human."

"He?" Father Fuselli asked.

"Yes. There were fingerprints and DNA left behind. Totally inconclusive other than to indicate gender. This is a photo taken from the camera footage."

On-screen was shown a grainy image of a man's face with thick eyebrows and messy waves of blonde hair, thinning perhaps? Cleft chin. Otherwise, he was nondescript.

"He stuck to the shadows." Father Manneli noted. "The rooms all remained dark because he didn't trip the door sensors. None of the door censors."

"Correct." said the Cardinal.

"Then how did he get in?!"

"Through the looking glass…" Magnus was muttering.

"Do you have something to offer, Father Magnus?"

"Not as yet. A portal would have required tremendous energy. A manifestation would have brought the smell of sulfur or ozone. This appearance has none of the common hallmarks of the usual forms of teleportation."

"Go on." he prompted. The Cardinal was always impressed with this one.

Father Magnus approached the view screen, peering closely at the angle of the footage.

"Look at the screenshot." He raised his hand to point at the lectern in the photograph. "Zoom back out."

The full view of the room telemetry had captured appeared. It was slightly skewed.

"There," he pointed at a dark object jutting from the bottom of the screen. Its flat surface was out of focus in the extreme foreground. "Who analyzed this?"

"Our finest techs did with minute scrutiny." The Cardinal was becoming even more impressed.

"Yet they succeeded in missing this." He turned and pointed, triumphantly, at the security camera. Its array of censors winked at him from the corner of the ceiling.

"He wasn't standing at the lectern." He gasped. "He wasn't even in the room!"

6. Driven Like the Snow

The drive to Dunkirk was devoid of conversation. Claura was at the wheel. Her focus was entirely on the road, eyes forward as she navigated our future.

She was in complete mission mode. I'm not sure what I expected. A leisurely cruise through the country?

Time and time again, she was breaking all my conventional thoughts on how women were supposed to work. I know I had only known her for two days, so I couldn't be a reliable judge. I was getting a glimpse of her other side, again, and it occurred to me that this was the norm for her. I was just part of an existence she never had a chance to explore.

Looking over at her again, my heart went out to her. I felt like a child wanting something for someone else and too stubborn to realize they might not want it.

She had her mission. After a childhood like hers, it was a miracle she was free to enjoy it.

Did she enjoy it? Again, I felt that pang. There were things in her life preventing her from having a normal one. I struggled to identify my feelings about it, about her. All I felt, now, was envy.

The monster, obviously, consumed more of her attention than she would ever let on. The mission had consumed her soul her whole life. I knew she didn't want anyone feeling sorry for her, so she kept it to herself like I forced myself to do right now. Laying my head back on the seat, I turned to watch her some more.

I could tell it was a comfort for her, just me being there. It wasn't just about the company for her or that she finally had an ally in the chase. Someone looked at her with adoring eyes, who weren't scared away by her obsessions. I was in it for the long haul.

I wasn't going to ruin it by trying to explain that to her just to pass the time and fill my void. I had to accept the fact that I was here, after all. That would have to suffice at times like these.

It would be petulant of me to crave her attention every stinking moment. I guess that was what I wanted so badly, for her to pay some attention to me this moment, not on where she was driving.

I longed to have her look over at me with those smoky eyes again, with that intensity she threw into everything. I secretly thought it was absurd of me. She had her whole life without me.

I added the road to my list of jealousies and moved on.

I turned my head to look out the passenger side window. Houses sped by in slow motion nestled in the trees. I couldn't help but picture all those vulnerable families. In every home, I imagined the Blood Banshee foisting his presence and having a field day. Each place represented another pen of innocent prey ripe for the slaughter. *This isn't helping*, I thought.

Gradually my head nodded. The smooth motion of the speeding car was lulling me to sleep. I decided to let it happen. Claura might be used to this level of activity, but he needed to be rested if he was going to be of any assistance.

He usually didn't remember his dreams, at least not after the few moments it took for him to awake. Maybe it was the drive and the awkward sleeping position. He was fully prepared to have nightmares in light of what was going on. Instead, he dreamt something about Seal Team Six or something.

In his dreamscape, a paramilitary group was rappelling onto a roof, laying siege to a fortress enclosing tunnels of gilt and glass.

Claura's mind was racing faster than her Rav4 as she took to the interstate. Her thoughts were broken up into multiple threads.

Part of her attention was on the road and their route. Another part was on the Blood Banshee and what they stood to learn about it. She was also using this time to reflect on her feelings for this man dozing next to her in the passenger seat.

She had never afforded any time to relationships. It was too hard to find anyone she could relate to. She had a problem with just touching people. Her encounter with that monster left her with more than just scars on her left arm and the scars on her psyche.

Besides the occasional bloody nightmares, some of which had had her screaming as she woke, she came away from his foul grip with a potential to see into people's minds when they touched.

That spelled disaster for most men that came into contact with her. Given her hot appearance and cool, mysterious demeanor, she couldn't tolerate a man's thoughts shouting in her head the things that were already evident on their faces.

She was more than satisfied with the looks in passing.

When she met Jack, she felt all those girlish notions of unicorns and love at first sight. She knew it wasn't like her, but it was clean and good. Everything life was supposed to offer two normal people.

There it was. Normal. It was something she thought was unattainable for someone like her. She had defended the rights of others to be at such liberties, fought for them, even.

It was a god-given right. She knew that. It was always a matter of self-sacrifice to her that she give up her place in that line. Nobody came away from the ordeal of her childhood without being changed. It was, almost, universally for the worst. This was her way of keeping grounded. It was the dedication that kept her out of trouble and out of the psych ward. She had to come second.

Then this guy comes along. She looked over at him in admiration. Not everyone would think he was much to look at. But he had an innocence that drew her like a moth to a flame.

Everything about him spoke to her as a man who didn't think he had a chance. It was refreshing to have that come off a guy. It was also an unspoken challenge to her to prove him wrong. And the sex, well, their first night, was better for that quiet insistence that he please her instead of thinking, solely, of getting his own satisfaction. That was unheard of in her experience.

Such a sweet man. She would make this world a safe place. If, for nothing more than to be able to have a normal life with Jack, she would regain his innocence by destroying this thing. Then they could walk, together, off into the sunset.

She had put everyone else first her whole life. Now, it was her turn.

As for the Blood Banshee, things had quieted down for years, now. She didn't know if it had to do with the distance between them. After all, he was roughly a whole continent away. She suspected it had more to do with the ease of access to his latest slew of victims.

He hadn't changed his location in almost seven years. She still got brief impressions of his whereabouts. In her dreams, she walked through glittering hallways of ultraviolet vines mirrored glass. And was that the walls of an Aztec temple?

All she knew was that he was content. She could feel that, and, without the ferocity of his past attacks, her dreams were, blessedly, less intense.

They had more to do with the meandering passageways that seemed to grow ever greater as if, somehow, his presence was causing the whole place to grow, spreading forever outwards.

Worse than that, previously, the horrible years of her nightly abductions into his murderous rampages were accompanied by the haunting images of his helpless victims. Now, she found herself walking the endless halls of the Arizona Mirrormaze accompanied by the souls of all the children he had consumed.

They crowded around her, their arms reaching to her for a release she was unable to provide.

It was maddening.

Their tiny hands would brush against her, and she would feel all the anguish and pain of their gory demise, as well as the joys they missed of the short lives from which they were, so brutally, cut off.

That was the hardest thing for her to cope with, reconciling those bright, innocent lives full of hopes and dreams with the mangled little corpses that followed her in droves, moaning and imploring with their blood-drenched hands.

Some mornings, she woke, remembering those lives so vividly she didn't know who she was. Then the guilt would crash down on her for not being able to help.

The reasons for payback only kept growing.

She wiped her eyes and kept on the 90 West. Eventually, they passed through Syracuse and Buffalo. As she homed in on their destination, she could see Lake Erie over her right shoulder. The coastline was no more than fifty feet away in places. She sped past the mailboxes of those houses set like pearls on the necklace of green grass and skeletal trees, their fallen leaves churning in their wake.

The horizon huddled close over the whitetops and chop of the water. It seemed to loom over the drifting homes like it would peek in through the back door.

Claura marveled how the back yards all looked as if they were, entirely, water. The edge dropped off, no more than twenty paces behind each house.

Distant capes thrust their tree-covered backs at the overcast sky. From the road, she could see how high, far above the water, their points dangled. Claura longed to visit one such promontory to sit on that edge and dangle her feet much the same.

She looked forward to a time when she might have a chance to do something as innocuous as communing with nature. She took a pull on her travel cup; the soda long turned to syrup.

They had less than a mile to go.

7. St. Columbans on the Lake

Claura gently shook me awake. I came to with a start totally unproportionate to the situation. It was dead silent. Given the destination, it might not have been wholly appropriate a phrase.

I shook the afterimages of special forces assaulting a glass labyrinth from my mind, rubbing the last of them from my eyes, and yawned.

Claura looked down at me from outside the car like I were a baby panda or, certainly, something as cute. I got myself together and looked up.

I was confronted with a Gregorian edifice, the likes of which I never imagined. Crenelated brick and vine choked mortar greeted my scrutiny with a happy warmth all its own. Stepped out of the car onto a gravel drive, mouth open in wonder at the immaculately tailored landscaping.

I suddenly felt like retiring. This place was a far cry from the ramshackle bones of my stifled harbor town. It was both ancient and new at the same time. For a converted monastery, it looked like it had just been finished yesterday. I drank in every inch.

The approach to its entryway was the last nondescript portion of my day. We stepped across the threshold and left the outside world behind.

In the enormous foyer, a kindly, a heavyset black woman greeted us. She was dressed the way a modern nursing assistant should. Her smile of welcome was genuine.

"Good afternoon. Welcome to Saint Columbans. My name is Ms. Martha. Can I direct you to whom you are here to visit?"

Her poised tones were educated in their delivery. She simply radiated calming patience.

Claura took the lead. Stepping forward, she shared Ms. Martha's handshake.

"My name is Claura Roberts." I took her hand next.

"Jack Lawrence."

"Well, don't you make a pretty pair." She folded her hands across her middle. Her knowing smile was like a promise of Christmas.

"We would like to see a Mister Bruce Horowitz," Claura was saying. "If we may."

"Well, I don't see why not. He's over in the east wing. This time of day, you'll find him in his room. He takes a nap right after supper."

"Can I offer a tray of coffee, or would you prefer tea?"

"Coffee would be great. Thanks." I said.

Claura could have gawked at their surroundings if she weren't on a mission. The monastic furnishings of this place were gorgeous. As they were led through a second courtyard, complete with lush gardening and religious statues, she resolved to retire there if she lived that long.

Elderly people roamed the place like tourists. They watched them go by with polite interest, looking on the pretty couple with proprietary smiles.

Down a medieval hallway were doors to some living quarters.

"Mr. Horowitz is in here." Ms. Martha said. "I'll be back with that coffee in a jiffy."

They peered into the doorway. A round little man sat in the corner near a love seat with a blanket over his knees. His salt and pepper curls matched his tight goatee. He set down his book and his reading glasses, gracing us with a solemn look.

His voice, when he spoke, was raspy as a chain-smoker's.

"Well. Come in. I've been expecting you." he lisped.

117

Chapter 2
The Gayle House Ghoul
Private Air Space
Stealth Military Aircraft
Altitude: 35,000 Feet, Mach 2

Magnus sat back in the sofa chair and stared, unseeing, past the tablet in his hands. He wasn't looking at the rich furnishings of the cabin. They held no allure for him. He had never been one to give in to the pride or the avarice that engendered such extravagance. He only appreciated the gesture it represented.

It was the thought that counts, they say.

The vast fortune of his patrons, The Roman Catholic Church, could afford the very best of the weapons and technology society had to offer. Restricted airspace and supersonic spy planes, aircraft with vertical flight capability that could stop on a dime, all their equipment was experimental by the standards of other countries. The United States, itself, didn't come close to their level.

The Holy Order of Saint Michael was more secretive than any other countries' organizations. They functioned outside the jurisdiction of the United Nations and their security council. They answered only to their own Papacy and to God.

Under them, all command decisions were placed solely with him. He was mission commander. He alone held the highest authority for the lengths they would go to enact God's will. If Magnus wanted to call in a nuclear strike, it was within his power.

Focusing back on the screen, he poured over, once again, the pages from the Book of the Ghoul. He strived to find something he could make use of. There was precious little there.

What they contained, though, he had to admit, was gorgeous in spite of their subject matter. Beautifully illuminated, the pages were a detailed account of the vile entity they were about to face, including its known capabilities. There was even an illustration.

The parchment yielded its timeworn surface to the colored ink, which looked so fresh it appeared to rise from it in loops and swirls of the fancy script. Accented with genuine gold, both pages were bordered with floral vines.

It was a masterpiece of art. The story it told was quite the opposite.

Not quite as intangible as a disembodied ghost, it was still more metaphysical than the average man-eating ghoul. Commanding less mystical powers than the boss vampire, it shared appetites with; it assumed only one form; that of a scaly blue primate with reptilian features, such as its eyes and fangs. It wrapped its terrible form in funereal raiment like the Scottish Banshee of legend. It wore an actual burial shroud like a grim white reaper.

And reap it did. The Blood Banshee raked its victims with retractable claws of indeterminate length that dripped a venomous paralytic agent. It subdued its prey in this way to make up for its lack of speed. It also made use of supernatural means of travel to surprise its intended dinner—this where the manuscript became vague.

It didn't utilize the shadow realm to move outside normal space like a Bogart. It was of a variety of night terror, like the kelpies and sirens of Irish and Greek mythologies, who were known to appear in bodies of water when one looked at their own reflection.

Other related creatures of the species were given names to familiarize people with their methods and appearance. The names of Jenny Greenteeth in Brittania and Nelly Longarms were passed down through folklore while the Blood Banshee's had not. It was very seldom to be seen in eyewitness accounts. Magnus wondered how often the others were mistaken for it.

Or it must be so successful as to leave few survivors to tell of it. The Boogeyman was heard of by everyone, but it moved through the interconnected Darkness and shadows, arriving at his victims from out of the closet or under the bed. The Blood Banshee moved through a realm behind ours, accessed through any reflective surface. Magnus had to classify it as an extradimensional being.

This thing was as old as time. Sightings dated back to the dawn of primitive man and their fear of the unknown. It was speculated that God, himself, had created this beast after the murder of Able by Cain to punish the wicked and scare the rest into line. For a time, it actually worked. Its hunger for children kept the population at a minimum, and there was peace throughout the growing nations and virtually no war. They were simpler times.

"Commander." his reverie was broken by Father Clovis. Magnus respected him for his martial prowess, which was augmented by his penchant to see into any situation more than was normally apparent.

Rivaling the prognostications of the Savants, Magnus accepted his unique ability entirely because they were a gift of the Spirit, the gift of certain knowledge. At any given time, Father Clovis would know with certainty useful details, answers to questions, or insider information. It was an unconscious thing for him. He hardly realized he did it. But, where most people had hunches or logic, Clovis had full knowledge, and he never failed to share it.

It was for this reason Magnus did not let him see the picture postcard that was found of the Mirror maze. It was that object that had burned out the Savant's mind, right after driving him to murder. He needed Clovis by his side for as long as he remained mission capable. This was going to be a tough one.

"What is it, Clovis?"

"The Cardinal was frightened. I've never seen him frightened before."

Magnus always saw one of the drawbacks of being raised by a church and not a family. A part of you remains a child. A day comes when you realize that holy men are still only men. The awe of those you wind up serving becomes a fragile thing.

It was broken for him long ago when he was still a child. He had witnessed the Cardinal in an event which humanized him for the lad. He no longer seemed infallible. Even as young as Magnus was, he recognized that. It turned out for the best. In a few years, He had come of age and looked on the Cardinal as he would a real father, someone whose safety and authority was to be cherished.

It healed over time. It was broken for Clovis, now, perhaps permanently. He may not live long enough to reconcile it like Magnus had.

"And this disturbs you?" he asked, not kindly. Clovis took his leader's tone as a command for attention.

"No, Sir." He straightened up quickly. Magnus gave him that. Clovis was the one he always had to steer right before a mission. The others blindly followed without ever knowing it was a luxury.

"What insights did you gather from the briefing earlier?" Magnus hadn't had time before they boarded to access his special perceptions.

"The evidence proved the intruder was just a man, but he's able to move around in the outer dimensions same as the target. A victim who survived an attack, perhaps?"

Clovis was hitting it on the nose, as Magnus expected. "And?"

"And, if it was a child who got away."

Brother Fuselli chimed in. He was our Information Tech on the team.

"I ran the address in Norwich. It corresponds with the beginning of this beast's trail of known missing persons. We traced the first family that disappeared to only three houses away. It's been owned by a family by the name of Lawrence for almost six generations."

"In its fourth generation, circa 1976, Ben and Martha Lawrence reported the disappearance of their eldest son. The boy's name was Henry. The case was never solved."

"The Oh Henry bar. How sweet. Good workmen. It seems like our mystery man was attempting to tip us off and none too soon. The Cardinal informed me as we left. There is such trouble our target is brewing that it is dangerously close to causing a rift."

"A rift?" Fuselli asked.

"Yes," Magnus added. "Between our world and, who knows, what dimensions."

"What would happen if it succeeds?"

"Any number of things." Clovis was shaking. "The dead could rise. Demons could spread abroad. All sorts of Cosmic Horrors!"

"The end of the World." Magnus sighed. They had all gathered around him.

"Here we go again." There was a call over the intercom.

"Commander, this the pilot. ETA fifteen minutes."

1. The Story Teller

Dunkirk New York
Saint Columban On The Lake
Room 101
8:00 Pm

"Come in, darlings." that voice rasped. "It's perfectly safe."

He looked us up and down from the corner.

"You're late. I knew this day would come, but I didn't expect it would take so long. Or that you'd be so cute!"

Claura took her usual cue. "I've heard that before."

"Not you, sweetie. I was talking to your man!" Out of the three of us, I couldn't tell who was blushing more.

Ms. Martha came in and set down a tray of coffee. "Will there be anything else, Mr. Horowitz?"

"No. Thank you, Martha." Then turned his wizened gaze back to us. Claura and I settled in and let him take the lead.

"I suppose you're here about the record. I did tons over the years, but there's only one you could be here about. Am I right?"

"The Gayle House." I heard myself say.

"The Gayle House," he confirmed with a solemn nod of his head.

"I was a freelance recording engineer when I was young. Before I got a job with MCA, I even had my own equipment. It was old-fashioned, a single unit, totally analog, y'know? You just stood in front of the bog ol' horn, and I'd crank the turntable by hand. The master was really soft, and the stylus would carve away. I had to wipe off the dross as it piled up."

"Anyway, that master would be sent to a manufacturer who pressed the copies. I never found out how. I just did the recording."

"My rig was totally portable. It wasn't much bigger than an old phonograph. I guess it the perfect setup for where we were. We'd been told to meet at an old abandoned house. Me and a sound effects guy and two others, some guy with his kid."

"There was no electricity. Real spooky."

"I'd answered an ad to do a haunted house record. Nothing like that had been done before, so I thought it would be a real kick."

"The guy that answered that phone sounded real cultured. He had a real rich-sounding accent, y'know, with a really deep voice. Anyway, he hired me on the spot, no questions asked. He just gave me an address for someplace way out in the country. He said he knew it was a long drive and that I would be 'compensated' for my trouble. He was already paying top dollar for my services, so I thought, what the hell? Right? For a quick, ten-minute job, I stood to make a whole lotta money."

"And to be a part of something that was never done before, my ego said it was perfect. It might be my shot to move up into the big leagues."

"Was I ever in for a surprise?"

2. Scare Record

An Abandoned House
Somewhere In Upstate New York
May 20th, 1969

The sun was threatening to set as Bruce Horowitz, recording engineer, bounced along the unpaved road. His gear rattled around in the back seat. For the umpteenth time, he hoped it wouldn't get damaged. It was pretty sensitive stuff.

Finally, the abandoned house hove into view. It sat on a hilltop next to a big, dead tree. The wood line was in silhouette all around, forming a natural clearing. It was like all the other trees in the area knew something about that house and couldn't stay far enough away.

It gave Bruce a chill that had nothing to do with the weather.

It was late October in the state of New York. Autumn had fully set in and wasn't going anywhere.

Two other cars were parked in front of the house as he drew up; a Ford truck and a station wagon. Hoping he wasn't late, he parked by them, grabbed his gear, and ran inside.

The interior of the hovel was more habitat than habitation. Every surface was worn. The wood that remained to construct the place was laid bare to a uniform brown.

Voices could be heard coming from the top floor. Bruce got up his nerve, spoke a prayer, and started up the rickety staircase.

The steps held long enough for him to reach the landing, but they had, surely, announced his presence. They'd creaked and groaned like a ship in a gale.

"Bruce Horowitz, sound engineer," he said by way of introduction. He lifted up his equipment to accentuate the claim before setting it down on a rickety table.

"Jean Shepherd." the sound effects man said. He was sitting by a stack of odds and ends; a couple of empty bottles, a baseball bat, a stick, and a glass window pane. Two empty chairs sat nearby.

Other than that, the only furnishings the room had to offer was a single, full-length mirror attached to the deteriorated wall. It was grimy like it was the old house's sole, longtime resident.

"I'm Gordon Winslow, and this is my boy, Arthur." We'd all shook hands and run out of things to say, so Bruce took it upon himself to break the silence.

"And where might our client be?"

Appearing out of shadows behind us came a tall man in an impeccable black suit and tie. The flared collar of his redshirt was positively diabolical.

"Good evening. I am Mr. Hobbs."

The gathering all jumped at his arrival. They had not heard a car pull up, nor had the creaky stairs announced his presence.

But for them, the room had been empty of occupants.

"I am Mr. Roarke, your host." Bruce joked under his breath, recovering himself.

"Allow me to introduce my associate."

Stepping into view behind him was the ugliest creation ever to set foot on God's green Earth.

Mr. Hobbs was taller than any of us, but this thing absolutely towered over him.

Wrapped in a full white sheet, his blue face identified him as an unnatural creature. Crazy yellow eyes glared hungrily from its beetled brows over a skeletal nose. From its mouth sprouted a cluster of fangs like enormous vampire teeth. The tusks dripped saliva onto the worm-eaten floorboards.

Bruce thought it was a fabulous costume.

"Rory, say hello to the nice people."

'Rory' didn't speak a word. He just breathed audibly. His gaze was fixed on the little boy.

"Shall we begin?" Mr. Hobbs asked. "I believe you have all received your lines?"

All were enraptured by this demonic duo, but something about the gentleman held them in more fear than the ape-like creature that loomed behind him like henchman enforcer.

"Mr. Horowitz. If you would be so kind."

But he didn't say it quite so kindly. If Mr. Hobbs had held a shotgun on them, he couldn't have been more intimidating.

Bruce began cranking. Jean was at the back of the room, and he opened a door. The tortured hinges ripped the air with a tremendous sound, and he played it out for as long as he could. Dragging a foot, he shuffled back over.

Gordon began speaking the first line in a ghostly drone.

"Do not be afraid, I have come from the world of the unliving to warn you."

Bruce listened in awe of this devilish show of epic claptrap. He hadn't seen the script and was secretly glad. He marveled at the cheapness of it all.

What the hell was a Blood Banshee, anyhow?

At the cue for its entrance into the tawdry serial, the beast let out a blood-curdling roar that had Bruce, suddenly, pissing in his pants right where he sat. Luckily, he was professional enough not to skip a beat.

This went on for a few minutes. The boy screamed to simulate two separate boys being eaten. Jean got right up into the megaphone and pretended to slurp their blood.

He rattled the chairs and broke the bottles for the fight scenes. At one point, he smashed the windowpane with the hammer. "It's trying to get out the window!" he yelled.

Then, it was time for the final battle.

"The stake, stake. Give me the stake!"

He proceeded to hit the baseball bat with the stick, accompanied by Rory's howls.

Once. Twice. Three times. A fourth. The beast's howls dwindled. It stepped back into the shadows and seemed to vanish.

Then the final line. Gordon pretended to be dying.

"It's days of evil are over. The Blood Banshee is dead. Uuuuuh."

That was it. Thank God that was over.

Jean followed Bruce outside for a cigarette. There was a real chance of burning the place to the ground. They chatted and joked about the carryings-on in there. Afterward, Jean made to leave, and Bruce went up to retrieve his equipment.

When he reached the top, something stopped him in his tracks. The creature must have returned. It wasn't a man in a costume, after all. His first clue was the way it was feeding on the body of the little boy.

Mr. Hobbs was standing nearby smiling a proud smile. He turned his grin on the horrified sound engineer.

Bruce looked around and saw Gordon. The boy's father was trapped behind the mirror's glass, pounding frantically on it like he was trying to get in a window.

Bruce looked back in shock at the distinguished gentleman. One flash of red from Mr. Hobbs's eyes was all it took to prompt him. All thoughts of his recording equipment and his pay went out the door. He couldn't follow fast enough as he made his narrow escape.

A lifetime went by, and he never forgot that session. Never breathed a word of it, either.

Sleep was a battle. He had reoccurring nightmares of a hellish, blue beast. Every night, he awoke in terror, expecting to be visited by that horrible fiend. He got used to lying on sweat-soaked sheets.

Time wore on, and there was no word of the scare record or the killer creep. He wondered if there would ever be a need to tell his story at all.

He waited, almost fifty years. Then the time had come.

Scottsdale, Arizona
Odysea Resort Mirror Maze
Altitude 500 Feet
2100 Hours

Magnus directed the aircraft in under stealth mode once the attraction had closed. The whisper of the vertical jets reached him through the open hatch situated under the fuselage just behind the glowing square of the thrusters.

With the silhouette of a small jumbo jet, he didn't expect they'd get much attention from below as they hung, aloft, in the darkness. This part of America boasted the largest portion of sightings of unidentified flying aircraft in the world. They would just have to risk one more.

"Base Camp, this is Archangel Leader. We are assaulting the objective. Maintain constant surveillance on the house until we get there. Do not move in without my direct order. Do you copy? Over."

"Copy that, Archangel. Over."

"Pray for us. Archangel, over and out."

With that, he plummeted into space.

Magnus was the first to fast-rope down ahead of his team as they descended through the Arizona night.

One by one, they hit the rooftop. Setting up a tight perimeter, they covered Brother Fuselli as he tapped into the building's security grid.

"Clear," he said in moments. "We have emergency lighting. All alarms have been cut, and surveillance set to loop."

"Good work, Fuselli. Men," he turned to his group. "I don't need to tell you to be careful. We go in hot and keep a tight formation. Circled up and back to back. No stragglers. We aren't splitting up under any circumstances for this one. Got it?"

"Roger that!" Their replies came in unison.

"Good. Fuselli, get the door."

The circular fuse burned a man-sized opening through the roof. The Pope would cover the cost if the building survived. They went down in the same order they had left the aircraft.

They formed up on Magnus. It was like stepping into the seventh level of Hell. Everything was lit up bright red. Corridors echoed each other, fading off in every direction. They picked up a pace they could keep, weapons up and aiming, as they stalked towards the center of the structure.

Deep inside the mirror maze, within an interdimensional pocket all its own. The Blood Banshee sat on a throne comprised of adolescent bones. He had sensed the intruders the minute they entered his halls.

With an evil grin, he stepped down and raised his arms. At his command, crowds of murdered school children materialized around him. He motioned them off, and they turned to disperse into the surrounding mirror frames, vanishing from sight.

They would provide the perfect distraction.

3. Gayle House

The Abandoned House In Upstate New York
9:30 Pm

After thanking Mr. Horowitz, we'd gotten up to leave. The dirty old man graced us each with a hug and a pinch on the cheek for our cuteness. I received mine on the buttocks.

Now, we jostled to the end of a long and winding dirt road. Bruce's directions had lead us, sure enough, to the lone figure of the derelict house. Its shadowy form rose up against the stars. A wreck of a station wagon rotted before it.

We had to have been the first visitors it had seen these fifty, long years.

I took the flashlight Claura offered me. She dug one out of the back for herself. I noticed she tucked her colt in her waistband, keeping it within easy reach.

We didn't say a word as I followed her across the crumbling threshold and up the moldy stairs. They still held our weight.

The room at the top greeted us with its deteriorated remains of tables and chairs. Broken glass littered the floor.

"This is definitely the place," Claura said as she crossed the floor. Bloodstains long turned to rust gave mute testament to its gory past. She approached the mirror.

Wiping away the grime of half a century, she stood there before it.

"I've never tried this before," she said.

"What are you going to do?" I stared in wild wonder as she reached a hand towards the surface of the glass. It passed right through!

Turning to look at me, she took a deep, ragged breath and stepped through the portal.

The room on the other side of the looking glass was an exact replica of the one she had entered from, only in reverse. It was just as solid. She brushed past Jack's reflection, making him shudder involuntarily.

Passing behind him, she looked down at the last resting place of Gordon Winslow.

His bones were laid out within the rotted fabric of his clothes. Whisps of hair still clung to his skull. Gaping eye sockets matched his open, skeletal jaw.

He had starved to death inches away from the edge of the glass.

Claura looked down for a minute in pity. Then she looked over at the opposite door. There was just one thing left that she had to know.

"Claura?" She could hear Jack's voice clearly as it entered the room.

"Come back, please!" He was getting scared. "What are you going to do?"

Without a word, she opened the door to look inside.

A yawning darkness screamed without a sound, right in her face. The silence was deafening. Air flowed past her as it was pulled inside.

There was a nothingness beyond the doorframe that stretched out into the void. It went on for an eternity.

The sucking breeze began to pull at her in earnest. Then there was an audible shriek, rising in volume and intensity. When it seemed like it wouldn't stop until it pulled her in, she slammed the door on it.

She had no intention of going in there.

Shaking with relief, she staggered back across the floor. It turned into a run as she dashed out and straight into Jack's waiting arms.

They trembled against each other for a long time.

I couldn't believe what I had just seen! Claura had walked right out of our reality into another dimension.

When she opened the reflection of that door, it almost got her!

"Don't you ever do that again!" I shouted.

Her only answer was to kiss me. She kissed me like a drowning person gulps for air.

"I had to know." she was muttering.

"How long did you know you could do that?!" I demanded.

"I didn't," she claimed. "But I suspected."

"It must have happened when that thing reached out of the mirror and touched you."

"All these years," she wondered, looking back over her shoulder. "What would it be like to live like that?"

Norwich, Connecticut
101 North Main Street
9:45 Pm

129

Bobby Whitaker was a precocious boy at the age of twelve. His parents were out for the night, and his babysitter was upstairs binge-watching some show on Netflix. The five families had the run of most of the house, so he and his ten-year-old brother Marcus were up late on a Friday night, playing hide and seek on the first floor.

They weren't allowed outside after dark. That was out of bounds anyway. They were safe, though, as long as they stayed in the house.

Marcus was counting out loud up on the first landing. Bobby looked up the stairs at him for a second to make sure he wasn't peeking. Then he went into the back living room to find his favorite hiding place.

The lights were on like they always were all night. Old man, Lawrence had a thing about the dark, even at his age. It made hide and seek harder, but Bobby wasn't thinking about that.

He was thinking about the little vinyl record in the dusty, white sleeve.

He found it on the floor in front of the stereo. The childish game was forgotten as he looked at the record than at the record player. He pulled the plastic disc out and looked at the label.

GAYLE HOUSE, it said in bold letters at the top. The bottom edge read Side One: The Haunting. There was a tiny picture of a ghost or monster reaching out with its claw. Its mouth was open, showing its fangs.

This should be good. A haunted scare record. This should scare the crap out of his little brother.

He lifted the clear, plastic lid on the turntable and put the record on.

He didn't know how to turn it all on, but as he reached out to open the glass door on the stereo cabinet, it took care of that for him. The stereo turned on all by itself.

He was too young to realize how scared he should be. He only glanced at the glowing LEDs until the spinning of the turntable drew his attention. The button on it pressed down, the stylus arm holding its needle came to life.

It slowly rose up and began creeping over.

Scottsdale, Arizona
Odysea Resort Mirror Maze
The Great Hall
Mission Time: 2135

Magnus had led his team of combat exorcists through the maze. Two minutes in, and shit got weird.

A cold mist was drifting across the floor.

"Contact!" Sax said on his right. The big man was aiming his AR-15 at the mirror.

Magnus risked a glance around his back and almost gagged. Deep in the mirror was the bloody vision of a little boy. It shouldn't be standing, given its level of maiming. But, stand it did. Worse yet, it was moving towards them.

In the red light, his blood was black. It covered him completely from head to toe.

"Over here, too!" Corelli barked from his left. It was the same thing, only this time it was a little girl. At least, it was most of one. He had to identify her as such from the bloodstained dress. She was missing her head.

That didn't stop her from taking another step right for them.

He shook it off fast. He had seen worse. They were just little kids, after all. What could they do? They were probably just ghosts.

"On our six!" That was Manelli. He was guarding their rear. "Multiple contacts!" He was starting to panic. "We're completely cut off."

"Keep it together, Excoriators," Magnus growled. But, when he looked back, he had to admit, it didn't look good.

A tide of gruesome, little corpses was flooding down the corridor right after them. They were closing in fast.

The way ahead was open so he began to sprint forward yelling, "MOVE, MOVE, MOVE!" They followed hard on his heels down the hall until it opened up into a grand chamber.

"This is the center of the maze." Fuselli had consulted the map on his tablet.

They stood in a wide room. Magnus estimated it was at least forty feet across. It was hard to tell from the mirrored effect of the walls. Pillars ringed with cushioned seating were set at regular intervals. It looked like a cathedral for a funhouse. In the red lighting, it was more like a madhouse.

That stopped as the regular lighting came on. In a flash, everything was blue and bright. Whatever was coming, sure wasn't afraid of the light.

He could feel it drawing near. Like a victim from a shipwreck, he was floundering, sure that there was a shark stalking him. He just couldn't see it yet and probably wouldn't until it was too late.

"Form up in the center!" he called out. "Face out!"

He struggled to remain calm. It was here. It just hadn't shown itself. It was toying with them.

"It's feeding off our Fear!" Clovis yelped.

Magnus led them in Prayer.

"The Lord is my shepherd! I shall not want! He maketh me to lay down in green pastures! He leadeth me beside the still waters!" They shouted at the mirrors around them. They used them to watch their backs.

"He restoreth my soul; He leadeth me in the paths of righteousness for His name's sake!"

A roaring sound began its call. It rose in counterpoint to their chanting.

"Yea, though I walk through the valley of the shadow of death, I will fear no evil." The howling got louder. "For Thou art with me; Thy rod and Thy staff, they comfort me."

"Thou preparest a table before me in the presence of mine enemies!"

"I've got movement!" Corelli pointed his barrel straight ahead of him. The blood beast had stepped into view deep within his mirror.

"Thou anointest my head with the oil!" He had taken the prayer back up, but the Blood Banshee was moving towards him. "My cup runneth over!" He was yelling.

"Surely goodness and mercy shall follow me all the days of my life," Magnus continued shouting at the top of his lungs, but he saw that every mirror held an image of the creature. They were converging on their little group of sacred soldiers. They were outnumbered twenty to one.

As he joined his brethren in the final line of Psalm 23, he braced for the monster's attack. He waited for them to emerge from the mirrors.

"AND I WILL DWELL IN THE HOUSE OF THE LORD FOREVER!" they chorused.

"Brace for it!" Magnus yelled. Only they didn't come out from the mirrors. He saw, too late, as the creatures all turned in unison on each Confessor's reflection.

He looked around him at his team. From out of nowhere, the bloody beasts had appeared right beside them.

"NOOOOO!" He had time to roar his denial once. Then he was shouted down by the screams of his men.

They were torn limb from limb. He could only watch in ever-growing horror as his team of Excoriators, the finest soldiers the mortal world had to offer, were butchered before his very eyes.

Each monster was huge, rising over Sax and Corelli like they were children. As they straightened from a crouch, one to either side of his men, two grabbed an arm, and one behind pulled off a soldier's head.

The lifeblood geysered from their necks as their craniums left them. Shoulders were gripped, and there was a Blood Banshee holding its mouth upon each neck, gulping it all down.

The others wrenched off the arms. They attached their sucking jaws to the empty sockets as they spurted the blood down their throats.

Only one Blood Banshee was left. It faced Magnus as he stood moaning. His anguish threatened to break his will as he began to lose his, once hard, mind.

He could only watch as the Beast stormed towards him. It reached out its paws, sinking venomous nails deep behind his body armor. They sunk into Magnus' ribcage.

He hung there in agony, and a paralyzing cold filled him to the marrow. He was helpless in the Blood Banshee's grasp.

Norwich, Connecticut
101 North Main Street
First Floor Living Room
9:46 Pm

The needle came down on the record. The volume of the speaker system had turned itself all the way up.

The howl of the Blood Banshee hit the room like a runaway train crashing through the back door.

It was playing side two.

Bobby clapped his hands over his ears before he could think. Then he yanked the needle from the record.

Scottsdale, Arizona
Odysea Resort Mirror Maze
Central Hall
Mission Time: 2146

The fiend had Magnus at his mercy. Both claws were sunk into his ribs up to the beast's first knuckle. He looked down the jaws of death as they pulled him up to the creature's face. The yellow eyes of lunacy danced in his head as their gazes locked.

Magnus, paralyzed by its poison, desperately thought of prayer, commending himself to his Maker.

This was the end.

Suddenly, the killer cocked its head to one side as if he heard his master's call.

Throwing its enormous head back in a last howl of fury, it began to fade. Its roar faded with it as it disappeared.

The Blood Banshee had been pulled into the Void.

Magnus fell in a heap to the floor.

The Abandoned House In Upstate
New York
Second Floor
9:55 Pm

Everything was fine after Claura's little jaunt to the other side. We were kissing, sharing our relief when suddenly she pulled away.

"O-my-God." She struggled out. I thought she was gonna be nauseous. She clapped a hand over her mouth. She fell to her knees on the floor.

"Claura, what is it?" I was insisting. She started having a vision.

"The children!" She began moaning.

"Soldiers!" I stiffened at that one.

"What soldiers? Where?" I was down on my knees with her. I put my hands on her arms.

She looked me in the eyes.

"They are being torn apart!" Both her hands flung up to cover her eyes. They had no effect.

134

"THEY DIDN'T HAVE A CHANCE!" she was shrieking. I thought I was worried.

Then she flung her head back and roared like a panther boiling in oil.

I jumped to my feet when I saw both her eyes. They had turned a bright yellow with burning red pupils. Her jaws yawned wide, and her teeth appeared sharper.

Her howl grew deeper in timbre. The volume shook the rafters.

In the haze of dust, Claura slumped forward in release. She pushed herself up from the rotting floorboards. I could see she was herself again. It still took a moment before she recovered.

"It's there," she said, eyes closed in languor or sorrow.

"What?" I asked.

"The Blood Banshee. It's back at the house."

I bent down to pick her up.

"C'mon. We've gotta go!"

Norwich, Connecticut
101 North Main Street
Third Floor
Bachman's Residence
10:20 Pm

Lucy Bachman had been awakened from a bad dream by a noise from downstairs. Sitting up in the dark, she pulled the covers up tight to her chest. She wanted her cat to comfort her and make her feel safe and snuggly again.

Mr. Jingaling was not in the usual place on her bed, though. She resolved to go find him.

Timidly, she crept from her room. She called for him quietly. She didn't want to wake Mommy and Daddy.

"Mr. Jingles," Lucy called softly. "Where are you?"

She entered their living room. One wall was an enormous mirror, reflecting the moonlight.

"Mr. Jingles…"

"Meow," came the diminutive reply. He was lost to her, somewhere in the dark.

"Where are you, kitty?" She looked under the couch. She thought she heard him there. Nope. Not there. Lucy turned on the light.

There he was, right behind the couch, cleaning himself with one dainty paw. He looked over at her and yawned.

"Meow."

That's when she realized. Lucy was looking at the cat beyond the backside of the couch. The couch had its back to the mirrored wall. Mr. Jingles should be in the center of the room, there beside her.

The kitten shook itself, trembling in fright. It was in front of the reflection of the couch!

Lucy knew enough to be sure that wasn't right. Still, she had to retrieve her kitten. It wasn't coming to her. It was scared and disoriented.

Carefully, she crept forward and slipped next to the couch. She stretched her hand out to the glass.

Her hand met no resistance.

Quickly, she sped to Mr. Jingaling and kneeled down to scoop him up.

"Poor kitty. Did you get lost?" she asked him, scratching his head.

Suddenly, the lights went out. She looked up in surprise with a short gasp.

Looking into the room, Lucy saw the closet door slowly open. The reflection of the closet door behind her squealed softly as it opened, too. Beyond it was darkness.

In a flash, a strange man darted to her side out of nowhere. He scooped her up like the kitten and dove out of the mirror.

Sprinting through the room, he headed out the door. Lucy screamed the whole way. Her parents met them in the hall, roused from their bed by their shrieking daughter. They flicked on the light.

"Who are you?!" they demanded, skidding to a halt. "What are you doing with our little girl?"

"Do not be afraid," Henry said.

"I have come from the land of the unliving to warn you. This place is haunted by a Blood Banshee."

"If you do not leave at once, each of you will die one by one!"

Chapter 3
Invite Your Friends Over
For A Haunting

Norwich, Connecticut
Rose City Auto Sales And Services
Vatican Military Base Camp
2235 Hours

The Holy Order's base camp was inside a tractor-trailer. It was parked, innocuously, in the auto sales parking lot across the street from the secondary objective.

Brother Honoria and Bucephalus were playing Call of Duty on the sofa. Brother Vestia was bringing a fresh latte to the fourth of their number, Brother Mingold, who was on shift. It was their job to provide constant surveillance on the enormous house.

"I think I've got something." Brother Mingold called out.

It looked like every single member of the household was streaming out the front door, down the front steps, and into the night.

It was cold in November, but they didn't have a care as something drove them out and into the street. They hadn't even taken the time to grab their coats.

"Stay here." Brother Vestia commanded.

"You two, start a pot of hot chocolate. Make it a big one. I'm going out there." He grabbed his parka on his way out the hatch.

Scottsdale, Arizona
Odysea Resort Mirror Maze
2240 Hours

Magnus was finally able to rouse himself. He was still shaky, and his lungs were filling with blood. At least the paralysis had worn off.

Pulling himself to his feet, he spat a mouthful of bloody phlegm and pulled up his radio.

"Archangel to pilot. Come in. Over."

"Pilot, here. We lost contact, Commander. Is everything alright?"

He was in no mood for explanations.

"Send down the line for one, through the roof. And set coordinates for Norwich. The second objective is in danger."

"Roger that, Commander. What about the rest of the team?" The pilot's tone conveyed his concern.

"The Excoriators are gone. Call in the Cleaners to mop up and give last rites. Archangel, out."

He took one last look around. The mist had receded. It looked like a slaughterhouse. He spared one, quick, moment to bow his head for his childhood comrades, then staggered off towards the rooftop access.

There was no time to lose.

He wanted to make that thing pay.

As Jack and Claura sped across the interstate, racing forever towards a horizon backlit by light pollution, their nemesis stewed in rage over its predicament.

For a brief moment, it had been an army. It looked back on the slaughter of the kill team sent to vanquish it.

He wished he could have savored the sweet victory a little longer. Their blood would have to sustain him.

He felt diminished. All the restless souls of his child-victims had been stripped from him.

He had taken the first steps to godhood. Now he was a cornered animal. For the first time in its eons-long existence, someone had knowledge of his presence. He needed something to tip the odds in his favor, again, if he wanted to destroy all of them.

He knew of a place nearby. He would need to procure transportation. But first, he would have to fight his way out to get there.

The Blood Banshee knew they would be coming for him soon. He hung back in the void beyond the closet's reflection, brooding.

He was going to make them all pay.

Norwich, Connecticut
Mobile Vatican Base
0700 Hours

Jack Lawrence Sr. stared at the stranger wrapped in the wool blanket. He huddled close to his tenants. They were all identical sporting blankets the priests had provided.

Everyone was either sharing a turn at playing Call of Duty, watching those who had, or finishing their sleep.

In the younger children's cases, it was the latter. Cots lined the inner walls of the trailer, and bunks were suspended above them.

Jack knew this man from somewhere. He recognized that teasing grin. He stared right back at him from across the room, smiling like he knew something Jack didn't, and he couldn't wait until the coin dropped.

Until that time came, he seemed content to blend in and keep his mouth shut. Shut on that infernal grin!

Brother Vestia was listening to his ear bead as he scanned the monitors. Standing over Brother Mingold's shoulder, he reported their progress to Father Magnus.

"Yes, Commander. The mirrors in the surrounding households are being blacked out as ordered. Break. We're using acrylic paint. It shouldn't cause any collateral damage. Break. Are you sure it will contain the threat? Over." He listened to his leader's reply.

"Affirmative. I copy your ETA as fifteen minutes. Base out."

"How is Father Magnus recovering?" Brother Mingold asked. "I heard the rest of his team was a total loss, and he sustained grievous injuries."

"You needn't worry about Father Magnus. The Confessors are enhanced for rapid healing." Vestia assured him.

Jack approached them and kept a respectful distance. These men were intimidating through the benefit of their obvious military posture. They wore black fatigues, yet, they talked like priests.

The level of comfort they, so quickly, doled out to him and his tenants were just astonishing. They did it with a softened touch and hushed voices that served to calm the others in record time.

There was too much that he found suspicious, though. And as the owner and landlord, the other adults deferred to him as their unofficial leader and spokesman. It was time he got some answers.

He walked up behind their leader and audibly cleared his throat.

"If you don't mind me asking, just who are you, people? What is all this? Have you been watching my house?"

"Mr. Lawrence, it?" Brother Vestia was glad to get the identification out of the way. "I can appreciate the confusion you must be feeling. Rest assured, we are only interested in your safety."

"If you have it in you to be patient for just a little longer, my superior is en route. He will be happy to explain everything."

"More than that, it is not my place to say."

Jack quietly fumed as he rejoined the others. A man so polite as that was hard to bitch at.

It was still dark out when Claura and I came to a screeching halt outside the house.

Before we could close the doors of the SUV behind us, we were greeted by a polite voice from the shadows across the street.

"Hello. I must ask that you don't go in there at this time. You'll be relieved to know, everyone has been vacated. They all got out safely."

"Who the Hell are you?" I asked. "How do you know what's going on here?"

"If you would, kindly, follow me, all will be explained shortly."

Claura shared a look with me and shrugged her shoulders. "Couldn't hurt."

We followed like he asked. He directed us to the side of a waiting semi-truck. Steps led up to a door in the side.

It was furnished like a parlor. Packed with all the family members, there wasn't much space left available.

My father was at the forefront of the group.

"Pop!" We exchanged the first hug I think I could remember.

"What's going on? Who are these guys?"

"Your guess is as good as mine. So far, they ain't talkin'."

"You see what happens when you leave the house? What have you two been up to, anyway? Do they have something to do with it?"

Once again, he'd struck too close to home.

"I don't know what you're talking about." I felt like a little kid again. He never failed to bring out the guilt in me.

Claura stepped up to smooth things back over. I felt a relief I'd never had before. She was a godsend. This was what it was like to have someone support you.

"Hi, Mr. Lawrence. Sorry, we were out so late. We had some work to do."

Pops was set back a pace, but I could tell he was in one of his moods. He must be worried about the house.

"Well, I sincerely hope you didn't bring this down on us, missy." Hoo-boy. Was he ever in rare form?

He even got Claura to look abashed.

I noticed over my dad's shoulder, a stranger had gotten up from the crowd and had come over. We shared an intense look with each other. Mine was bewilderment. His was a knowing smile.

Who the Hell was this? My father went from ranting at me to raving at him.

When he saw me looking at him, he swung his head back and forth between us. He whipped around on him so fast; I swear he wanted to deck him.

"WHO ARE YOU?!" He roared.

The man's smile just got wider. Through his teeth, he spoke.

"You don't remember me then, do ya, Jacky?"

2. The One That Got Away

Claura watched Jack's father turn as white as a sheet. He was whispering something as he fumbled back for a chair. I thought, for sure, he was having a stroke.

"Henry?" he whined. Something about this man had reduced this saw-bitten warhorse to the level of a weeping child.

I looked up at him. Everything about him was nondescript, from his thinning hair to his mismatched boots.

"Yes, Jacky. You do remember." he was saying slowly. He looked like he had enjoyed teasing the old man his whole life.

Then it struck her. She figured out who he was. Why, on earth, didn't she see the resemblance sooner?

"Do you have a brother, Mr. Lawrence?" she heard herself asking.

Both Jacks, junior and senior, wore matching looks of shock on their faces. It was Jack Jr's turn to grill his father.

"You never told me you had a brother."

He was really letting him have it.

"Why didn't you tell me? I had an uncle. *Have*an uncle. What is the matter with you! Tell me!"

His father just sat there with his face in his hands, shaking all over.

When he answered, it was to snap:

"Because I thought he was dead!"

The old bastard was back that quick. He pointed a finger at this Henry guy. He accused him with his entire arm.

"I WATCHED YOU DIE!" He had everyone else looking. Then he broke down in tears.

"I was five! Do you have any idea what that does to a child?!"

"It's alright, Jacky. Let it all out."

He pulled his younger brother in a sad embrace. He patted his back one-handed.

"I got lost."

Norwich, Connecticut
101 North Main Street
April 1st, 1975

"No, Jacky. I already told you. You get nightmares. And if Mom and Dad find out, they'll KILL me!"

Jack pleaded with his older brother.

"I SWEAR, Henry! I won't have nightmares. Just let me listen to a little…"

He idolized his brother. He dressed like him and wanted to like everything he liked.

"For the last time, NO!" He loved his little brother. But, sometimes, boundaries had to be set.

There was that one time Jacky tried to get him with his own joke goblet.

He had just gotten it in the mail. His growing collection of mail-order novelties was supposed to be off-limits.

Somehow, Jacky had gotten it in his head to try and fool Henry with it.

It was supposed to look like it was full of wine, and you act like you're going to spill it on someone. But, it's really a double layer of glass containing the fluid.

142

Jacky had snuck into his brother's room. He had walked up to Henry, the goblet hidden behind his back.

Only, when he went to *pour* it at Henry, it slipped out of his little fingers, shattering on the floor.

Jacky horrified at what he had done, just ran.

Henry didn't have the chance to either scold him or forgive him.

He'd bet the little jerk would be living with it for the rest of his life the way it stands, anyway.

He closed his door on Jacky's look with that bottom lip of his quivering, like, *mumumumu*. It wasn't gonna work this time.

It was Friday night. Their parents had gone out to an April Fool's party. They wouldn't be back till eleven.

Henry went to his chest of comics. His shelves were bursting with dime-store novelties. He opened the chest and took out the scare record.

Henry had just gotten it in the mail that day. He'd fallen in love with that monster in the ad. 'Invite your friends over for a…Haunting!'

He was determined to listen to this alone.

Henry opened his cheap, single speaker record player. He turned it on and placed the record on it.

Carefully, he placed the needle on the outer edge of the spinning plastic disc.

The roar emitted from the speaker, about, split his eardrums. He had put on side two by accident.

He didn't want Jacky to hear, so he tried to turn it down.

There he was, next to his mirror, struggling with the volume knob.

The next thing he knew, the creature from the ad popped up in the mirror!

Henry screamed his head off as the thing reached out from the mirror and grabbed him.

"Henry! Henry!" Jack pounded on the door. He tried the doorknob and burst in.

He watched in terror as his older brother's feet kicked and kicked, sticking out of the hole in the wall.

"Wait!" he yelled and went to the mirror. All he could see was a big guy in a white hood, grappling with his brother.

Jack looked over and grabbed Henry's baseball bat, determined to save him.

He swung it once.

The bat connected with the mirror, smashing it to splinters. The spiderweb of cracks filled the frame.

When his parents returned home, they found every light in the house turned on and little Jacky, curled up alone, in his brother's room crying. Henry's baseball bat was still in his hands.

At first, they thought their eldest son was playing a cruel prank on his younger brother.

After hours of searching, they still weren't laughing. His mother was in tears as his father called the police.

"We looked for you EVERWHERE!" Jack was blubbering.

"Mom and Dad didn't believe me. They were convinced someone broke into the house and snatched you right in front of me."

"Oh, they were half right, but no therapist was ever gonna let me believe the truth."

"Let me tell you; there were plenty that tried. Ten years later, I had to tell them whatever they wanted to hear just so I could go home."

"I'm sorry." Henry tried.

"What the Hell happened to you?!"

It was Henry's turn to look ashamed.

"Well, when you smashed the mirror, it startled the thing, and I got loose."

"Then I ran. I kept running. I closed my eyes and made sure that thing wasn't gonna catch me."

"I must have been miles away when I came to my senses. I didn't know where I was or how to get back."

"I was in a supermarket. At least I thought I was. Everything was backward. All the writing on the food labels, cereal boxes, everything!"

"It's a good thing everything worked. I would have starved!"

"It took years to figure out how to get around. I lived in the reflection of that supermarket."

"I watched as everything changed. A newer supermarket was built with clothes and bedding. Even shotguns. I thought, wow, this tram law place is great!"

"But I had to see the outside world. I was able to get out, but the only place I knew to sleep was within. I slept in furniture stores after they closed or people's houses while they were at work."

"I stole anything I needed from out of the reflections. They don't get missed as much that way."

"I moved around a lot."

"I came out to take books and stuff in. I even robbed a bank one night."

"I paid cash for cars and plane tickets. Boy, I tell ya. Finding someone who looked enough like me to steal an I.D. from took two years before I got it right."

"By then, I'd watched a lot of cop shows, sitting right in someone's living room. I learned about fingerprints and security cameras. I figured out how to be more careful."

"I'd had a lot of close calls up till then. People always thought I was a ghost, though."

Jack wasn't having any of it.

"Why didn't you call? If you could travel, why didn't you come home to tell us you were okay?"

Henry stood up for himself.

"Because you guys would have freaked out. And I would've had to lead a normal life. I see how people've got it. Believe you me; I am not gonna live like some loser rock star on the Real World."

"Face it. People suck. They only demand things from each other. And when they don't, it's because someone already feels obligated enough to give it to them."

"Look at you, right now! Do I get a 'welcome home, Henry. Gosh, I missed you?' NO! It's all about you, you, you."

"I almost got eaten that night, for Christ's sake."

"By the way. I never got a chance to thank you for saving my life. Thank you."

Jack Sr. looked up from the floor, sufficiently chastened.

"You're welcome. I just wish you could have said it sooner."

"Yeah, well. If you'd had it made, I wouldn't have wanted to screw it up for you. By the time I was able to come home, the damage was done. Me showing up would only have made it worse."

"I'm sorry, Henry," Jack heard his dad say. "We're just gonna have to agree to disagree on that."

"Fair enough," his uncle said. Then he turned to me.

"Well, you don't look like you turned out too bad. You've got quite a woman, there, with you. Eh?"

"We just met," I said.

"Oh. Well, what have you been doing with yourself?"

I couldn't resist. "I stay at home. I sold your collection. Set the monster free, again. Y'know. Kid stuff."

The old man actually laughed.

"Well, you inherited a sense of humor at least."

3. Don't Delay Order Today

There was nothing more that needed to be said.

Our silence was broken by a rushing sound from outside.

Without thinking, I jumped for the door and wrenched it open. Claura was right there by my side.

In the pre-dawn light, we looked up at the miniature jumbo jet hovering just above the rooftops, deftly avoiding the power lines. A square, burning with internal flames, was the only light coming from it. It was, also, the only thing keeping it aloft.

It sat there, nearly silent, as a big rope dropped its end to the ground. Another man in black military gear slid all the way down it.

He stalked over to the trailer like he owned the thing. The aircraft disappeared from sight behind him before the sun could illuminate it.

He hit the top of the steps. Claura and I moved aside for him because he wasn't stopping. He was a big mother. Chiseled features and nazi hair marked him out as a genetic superman. He gave us a curt nod.

His boys had all snapped to attention.

"Peace be with you," he said in martial tones. It was like he said 'at ease' because that's how the soldiers reacted.

With a chorus of "And also with you." they went back to what they were doing.

The one who had been in charge stepped up to take orders. They conferred quietly, tipping their heads together for privacy.

At something his underlining said, he looked over his shoulder at my dad and then the three of us standing by him.

He walked over and offered a hand for shaking. He was obviously bred to be sharp, too. He knew who I was and got right to the point.

"Jack Lawrence Jr.?"

"Yes?" I grudgingly admitted.

"We want to thank you and your father for tolerating us. We know it's a surprise. But we have orders to safeguard your place and cleanse it."

"Cleanse it?" I found myself asking. "Cleanse it of what?"

"Why, of Evil, Mr. Lawrence. We ask that you quietly let us do our job, and things will be back to normal in no time."

"Like at the Mirror Maze?" Claura suddenly asked. She meant it as a barb, but I could tell she had meant something more by it.

Whatever they thought they were doing, she wanted in.

The man's reaction was priceless. About ten different emotions crossed his face in half as many seconds.

He straightened right up when he was done. Nodding in silence to himself, he came to a decision. He turned to address the crowd.

"If I could have everyone's attention, please." he began.

"I am Father Magnus of the Order of St. Michael, Vatican Exorcists task force."

"Your house is, currently, inhabited by a spiritual threat. We have everything under control. Once it is eliminated, you will be able to return to your home."

"Until then, I ask that you all remain here where it's safe. Thank you."

My dad spoke up.

"Are you saying my house is possessed?"

"No, Mr. Lawrence. It's not quite that complicated. This is a corporeal creature of flesh and blood. It can be killed."

He turned to his men.

"Brother Honoria, Brother Bucephalus. I believe one of their McDonald's is open nearby. Take their orders and take the van. Get these people something to eat."

Then he turned to Claura and me.

"You two, come with me."

He leads us to the storage lockers at the front of the trailer. He gestured for us to sit down and did the same.

Claura didn't wait for him to speak.

"You've come for the Blood Banshee, haven't you?"

"Please identify yourself," he commanded politely.

"Claura Roberts."

"Hmm," he said. "And, just, how did you know about the Mirror Maze?"

"She saw it." I piped in. "She's able to see what it sees."

"I see." He smirked at that, himself. Then he got serious. "Why is that, exactly?"

"When I was seventeen," she began, "it grabbed me. Here." She rolled up her left sleeve. Showed him her scars. "There was only one mirror in my house. It was too small for it to get all of me."

"It was able to get at others in my life, though. The killing spree was short. Only three dead. But I saw it in every detail in my sleep."

"Since then, I was forced to watch every time it attacked. I kept track of its location that way."

"I followed its back trail to this house where I met Jack. We've been learning what we can about it so we can stop it for good."

"And what do you think it is?" He asked.

"Well, we know what it is and where it came from, for one thing," I said.

He looked over at me. "You do?"

"It came out of an old scare record from 1971," I said. "We met the sound engineer that recorded it."

"Do you mean to tell me it's attached to a vinyl record?"

"Yes. My uncle, over there, played it back in 1975. It was trapped in the attic until I played the record again."

"It didn't attack me. It decided to leave. It's been going around, killing people, for the last twenty-five years!"

"I see." He was so damned calm.

"Do you really think it can be killed?" Claura asked. "I mean, look at what happened to you guys in Arizona! Do bullets even stop it?"

A dark cloud rolled over him. He looked at the ground, remembering a floor littered with his teammates' body parts.

"We never, even, got off a shot," he admitted in quiet regret.

"But there is one thing in our arsenal that is reported to do the trick." He was looking at Henry. "which reminds me."

He got up and walked over to him.

What did he want with my uncle?

"Henry Lawrence, I presume." Magnus had moved upon him like a hungry tiger.

He decided to feign innocence.

"Do I know you?" he blithely inquired.

148

"Come, come, Mr. Lawrence. I recognize you from the surveillance photo. I was very impressed. And those clues you have provided an invaluable service to us."

"Don't try and save me, Father. I was just looking out for myself."

"Undoubtedly." Magnus retorted. He leaned in conspiratorially. His voice was a mock whisper. "Do you still have it?"

In reply, Henry opened one side of his jacket. His other hand half pulled out an ancient wooden stake. He put it back like a crooked peddler with that insipid smile.

"Good," Magnus told him. "You're going to need it." He made was to walk away.

"What?" He was flabbergasted.

"You're going in with us."

"The Hell I AM!" Henry shouted, childishly.

"Why else did you take it, Mr. Lawrence?" Magnus turned on his heel.

"Only to protect myself!" His ego was taking a beating, at last.

Magnus aimed the last word over his back.

"Then why come 'here'?"

4. Be the First in Your Neighborhood

The chaplains had returned with breakfast. They all broke bread together. Magnus even said a prayer.

When they had finished eating, he called over two of his men.

"Brother Vestia, Brother Milford. Gear up. We're going in."

Claura stepped up behind him.

"What is it, Ms. Roberts?" He didn't need to look to know who it was.

"I'm coming with you."

"No, you're not," he said with deceptive softness.

"You're taking him!" She jerked a thumb over her shoulder at Henry.

"He can access its realm. We need the advantage." Magnus insisted.

Claura was even more insistent.

"Think. He can cross over because the Blood Banshee grabbed him. I've done it, too. He sunk his claws into you."

"That makes three. Enough of an advantage for you?"

Magnus considered it, looking down at his weapon. He looked up from under his eyebrows at her.

"Do you know how to use one of these things?"

Claura only looked at Brother Vestia at the weapons rack.

"Hit me," she said.

Brother Vestia tossed an AR-15 at her.

She looked him in the eye the whole time as she caught it one-handed by the upper receiver in her left. She turned the neck of the buttstock into her right hand.

That hand gripped the charging handle, and she drew it back, locking the bolt to the rear with her left thumb. She slid the lever back in with a click and automatically glanced at the open port and said, "Clear!"

She accepted a full magazine, slapped the back of it twice on her thigh, and slid it home in the magazine port. She slapped its bottom twice.

She released the bolt, and it chugged forward with a satisfying 'clunk.'

Thumbing the selector switch to safe, her fingertips snapped the breach cover closed.

She was locked and loaded. Her weapon was held at the ready, across her body, angled with the barrel pointed up.

Vestia and Milford shared a look; their eyebrows waggled up.

Magnus spoke.

"Get her somebody armor."

In the end, Jack pressed to go as well. Magnus handed out the wooden stakes to everybody.

"Blessed bullets might only hurt this thing. By all accounts, it can only be killed by one of these."

Jack looked down at the shriveled piece of wood. He could feel a power that belied its appearance.

"Where did these come from?" he asked in a trembling voice.

Magnus spoke with reverence.

"You have in your hand, my friend, a piece of the Holy Cross. Not some garden variety hawker's sham. This is the real thing."

"Jesus Christ." Jack breathed.

Magnus said, "Exactly."

I felt like I was inside a video game.

There we were, loaded to bear, and I get handed a magic item to level me up.

Pop was proud. I could tell by the glimmer in his eye as he threw an arm around me. Then we were out the door.

The sun had risen on Norwich with a golden weight that held down everything in sight. We went up the porch, and they showed me, real quick, how to stack on the door.

They'd put me in the middle.

Magnus took the other side so he could throw a flashbang in without bouncing it off the door.

"Close your eyes till I say 'go.'" He told us.

"Fire in the hole!" I heard the small device hit the floor. Then the 'BANG!'.

I saw the light through my eyelids.

Then Magnus yelled, "GO, GO, GO!!!"

We went. We went through half the household like that.

The power had been cut. Cut by the monster. That's why Magnus had waited until the sun was up. Dust motes swirled in galactic patterns in the streams of light.

He'd seen the floorplan before leaving the trailer. Still, it was a maze in its own right. Every square inch was filled with something valuable, and Magnus fancied he could see the memories of this place dancing in the sunlight.

"Keep your reflections out of any mirrors. It can attack you through them. That goes for any glass, too."

He kept throwing flashbangs at every corner. It was more to piss the creature off than startle or blind it. Magnus had to force it into making the first move.

The Blood Banshee was pissed. A band of humans had cornered him, at last. They had isolated the house from those around it. They had painted over those mirrors.

Now, they were foolish enough to walk within his reach. They thought they had him outnumbered this time. He still had a trick or two yet.

They should have brought more soldiers.

"It's like a scene right out of a poorly made slasher film." I was saying.

We had crept through the house for a good half hour. There was no sign of the thing.

"Claura," I whispered. I was right by her ear. "Are you getting anything?"

I figured she might see what it was seeing. If she could describe whatever it was looking at, that might tip us off to its location.

"Nothing. All I'm getting is darkness."

"Maybe it has its eyes closed." That came from Brother Mingold. Did these guys have a sense of humor, after all?

We were on the second floor. The last residence left to clear on this floor was the Bachman's. We went in through the door just like all the rest. A combat caterpillar of death.

We checked the kitchen and the front bathroom. We headed down the tiny hall.

Henry whispered at Magnus.

"There's a big mirror in that room." He was pointing his barrel at the living room.

The double doors were open.

"He's right," I said. "The whole wall is a mirror. It's behind the couch, on the left."

"Okay," said Magnus. "Here's what we're going to do." He looked at all of us.

"We're going to line up across from the mirror at the up and ready. Aim for the mirror."

"It's called a strong wall. Got it?"

That was for the benefit of us civilians.

"Roger." We said. We even said it together at the same time. I was getting good at this, I thought.

We hustled in and stood shoulder to shoulder. The couch was facing the firing squad. Do you have any last words? I crack myself up, sometimes.

We waited for a couple of heartbeats. We began to relax.

The closet door behind us exploded in a cloud of tinder!

The Blood Banshee burst out, barreling straight at the first person in front of it.

That just happened to be me!

I watched it in the mirror. Like a runaway train, it was bearing down at my back.

I did the only thing thinkable in situations like these. I ran in a circle!

I didn't want to run into its reflection, so I hung a left. It was no use. It hooked a paw around me and spun.

Wrapping me in a bear hug, it dragged me backward. We went right into the mirror!

"Jack!" Claura screamed. "NOOOO!"

Before anyone else could move, it was Henry that leaped at the mirror. He passed through before the Blood Banshee could drag his nephew out of sight.

He rammed himself against them. With the weight of them both, added by a combined three hundred pounds of body armor, he bowled the monster right over.

The three of them landed in a heap.

The Blood Banshee was pinned. Unwilling to relinquish his hold on Jack, it couldn't fight back as Henry pounded its face with his buttstock again and again.

"LET HIM GO!" He yelled.

When it did, Magnus and Claura grappled with its arms in an attempt to immobilize it.

They were all yelling, now.

Henry pulled his wooden stake from the webbing on the front of his vest. He held it up above his head with both fists, ready to plunge.

Jack was in the way, still pinned beneath him.

Jack threw both hands up.

"No, no, no, no, no!"

That moment of hesitation was enough for the beast to shake them all off. They fell in different directions.

By the time they could recover, it had escaped from the mirror and moved to the window.

On the way, it hurled Brother Vestia by the throat, tossing him into Brother Mingold. Then it swung one massive arm at the glass, as many times as it took for it to break.

"It's trying to get out the window!" Brother Vestia yelled.

Henry was the first one out of the mirror. He was, certainly, the hero of the day. He threw himself at the beast.

"It will not escape!" he roared.

He hit the Blood Banshee full tilt. They rolled over the lintel and on top of the porch. They continued to roll until they went over the edge and were lost from sight.

The rest watched from inside the house.

Magnus said, "We've got to get down there!"

It was a mad dash out the Bachman's door and down the staircase.

They caromed down the front porch, leaping the last few steps, and ran for the street.

The Blood Banshee was almost out of sight. It kept shrugging Henry off as he tried to drag the creature down. Once or twice, he drove the stake into its back. It was no use.

The thing had a hide on its back tough enough to deflect it.

Claura stumbled, and Jack was there to catch her. She had her hands on both sides of her head as she went to her knees. Jack knew what was going on in her head. Her link with the creature was active, again.

"Oh." Claura started saying.

"It's headed for the interstate," she said.

We all looked at where the two of them went. They were by the freeway, now. The beast pulled down the fence, stepped over the guardrail, and crossed the shoulder. It proved its intention to walk right into traffic.

Henry was clinging to its shroud. Then they vanished.

The traffic never, once, slowed down. The cars continued to zip westward "It's trying to get to Hartford." She gasped. "Jack, what's in Hartford?"

"Oh, no," I said. Then I grabbed Magnus by the arm. I told him, "We need to get to Hartford. Fast!"

"Why?" he asked. "What's in Hartford?"

"Look." I was getting desperate. "Just get us a van and call in some firepower."

"This shit's about to get real heavy."

154

Chapter 4
Days of Evil

1. The Battle on The Interstate

Norwich, Connecticut
Veterans Of Forever Wars Highway
75 Mph

The Blood Banshee had tried to make a clean getaway. Henry had held on tight as they fell to the ground. The crest of snow had accepted them with a three-foot drift to soften their landing.

They had continued struggling as they got to their feet. Henry had stuck with it as they took the battle to the freeway.

Half a block stood between Main Street and the Veterans of Foreign Wars Highway. The Blood Banshee had thrown Henry off time and again, every step of the way.

Claura and Jack had reached the edge of the street. Henry could hear them calling his name as the Beast made to leap for the speeding traffic.

They'd seen Henry cling to its shroud before they were both whisked away.

They just vanished.

Pulling himself close, they rolled around in the minivan they had entered, visible only in the rearview mirror.

Sheila Dunwoody was just a middle-aged mother of three. She was going to be late picking her children up from soccer practice. An invisible force seized the van and rocked it. Holding on tight to the steering wheel, she tried to identify the source of those sounds, heavy breathing and grunted remarks. What was that heavyweight in the back tossing her vehicle to and fro?

Looking over her shoulder in the back would have proved it was her imagination. The back was empty. Looking in the rearview to see if she were about to cause an accident made her think she was losing her mind.

Two guys were struggling with each other in the back seat. The man in black military fatigues was holding the wrists of the one wearing a bedsheet.

He was desperate to keep the other from sinking the pointed spikes on its blue alligator skin gloves into his face.

She almost crossed into the next lane after she got a look at its face. And it was an 'It,' alright. Pulling back, just in time, before she could hit the car beside her, She looked up again.

They were gone. They had taken the fight, and their jostling weight, elsewhere.

We shot like a rocket to Hartford. The VOFW was half slammed. Interstate 2, heading west, was just settling down after the morning commute.

We had taken two vans. The second one carried three of the soldier priests. Brother Vestia was at the wheel in ours.

The vans were all black without any insignia. The tinted windows hid our identities. This was total secret agent stuff. I'm sure nobody noticed us.

The way we were flying, I was surprised we didn't have the attention of the police.

Brother Vestia was doing his best Mario Andretti impression. He, mainly, drove on the shoulder. The other van stayed right on our tail.

The day drifted behind us without a care in the world. The usual traffic was content to pursue their own individual purposes, namely, driving twenty-five miles over the speed limit.

We were attempting to do that twice.

I looked around at the other cars as we passed them by. Nobody had a clue that anything was out of the ordinary.

I had to check that. I noticed, up ahead, a minivan was wobbling. It was all over the lane as if the driver was having trouble keeping it straight.

They almost collided with the car right next to it. Then it calmed down and was fine.

A sedan took an opportunity to pass around to the left. As they pulled up alongside, it seemed to suffer an invisible impact. It looked like something; either pushed it or pulled it aside a pace.

As we got closer, it rocked from side to side on its wheels. The driver looked in his rearview. He was shocked by whatever he saw. He almost lost it rubbernecking in his back seat.

I looked through the backdoor window and couldn't see anything to explain what was setting his vehicle off-balance.

I had a safe bet of what it was.

"There!" I said, pointing at it.

"Is that where they are?" Magnus asked.

"At the moment," I informed him. "They must be moving from car to car."

"Keep me posted," he said. He was busy on his tablet.

"Oh my God." Claura hissed. The sedan almost rear-ended someone. He managed to use the brake in time.

The truck in front of it stood its hind end up on its shocks for a few feet. I could see into its mirrors for a second.

The heads of our two prizefighters popped up in them for that split second.

It's like I looked through little peepholes into what was opposite our world.

Henry and the Blood Banshee were in it. They were going from car to car, duking it out, nose to nose.

"We have to get ahead of them!" I shouted at Vestia.

"You haven't even told me where we're going." Magnus opined.

I looked over at his tablet. Then I pointed at the navigation in the dash.

"755 Main street!" I spat.

"Oh no." Claura moaned. "I felt it. That's what it wants."

Magnus was perplexed.

"Look up 1 Financial Plaza," I told him, pointing at his tablet. "You'll get the idea. He had his claws in you. Can't you feel it?"

"Maybe he had me more recently, but either way, if I were him, that's where I'd go."

He looked at the information, scrolling on his tablet with a finger. He found the image. It was exactly what I imagined.

Then he opened a new page. He began looking up the nearest Guard regiment. Then he looked up the Army Reserves.

The combatants fought all the way across Interstate 2.

The Blood Banshee managed to kick Henry, getting both clawed feet under him.

Henry sailed from the car.

Fully in the mirror zone, he landed in a car that was traveling faster. He waited as it pulled alongside and dove headfirst into the killer's vehicle.

The fiend looked up, only to be tackled from the vehicle. They bounced right out, rolled up together in their dual death grip, and right into another car.

It went on like this for over an hour. Henry was starting to get tired. He would never let up, though. His desire for revenge on this thing that had stolen his life fueled him with adrenaline. His revulsion at its touch sent him into a manic display of superhuman strength.

He had to be the one to finish it.

The monster suddenly reared its head up. It had spied its destination.

Twenty-six stories, three hundred and thirty-five feet of shiny glass, reflected the skyscrapers surrounding it.

They were in sight of the Gold Building.

From top to bottom, all four sides were the same.

1 Financial Plaza was the biggest mirror the Blood Banshee had ever seen.

Its ugly face split into an evil grin that it turned on Henry. Ignoring his feeble attacks, it reached over the driver and took control of the wheel.

Bill Leeds was an assistant manager at the Financial Group. His office on the ninth floor was, normally, the only thing on his mind at this time of day; the 9 am traffic his only problem. At that moment, all hope for normalcy was gone. His only problem was losing his mind.

He'd already lost control of his Audi completely. His sanity soon followed as the Blood Banshee rose into sight in his rearview mirror. It was climbing over the front seat. Then he felt something push the gas pedal to the floor.

Henry was flung back as the car hurtled across traffic at top speed. It ran a red light, jumped the curb, and bounced across the sidewalk in an instant.

They crashed against the corner of the building. The car's owner, Bill, was saved by the airbag. No such protection was able to prevent the two mortal enemies from exiting the vehicle when it came to an immediate stop.

They sailed across the lobby in their own pocket universe, fetching up in the mirror surrounding the elevator.

Onlookers witnessed the two skid to a halt deep in the reflection of the foyer.

Henry had the wind knocked out of him as the Beast climbed to its feet. It stalked towards the edge of the mirrored wall. That sent the crowd running in panic at the sight of it.

It stepped out of the mirror.

As the humans scattered at his terrifying magnificence, he slowly raised his arms, palms up, in benediction. It was a promise of more to come.

He offered them Pandemonium.

Hartford, Connecticut
755 Main Street
1 Financial Plaza

The others could only watch, helplessly, as a white Audi cut its way out of traffic and increased its speed. It was aimed directly at the Gold Building.

At that time of day, there was a lot of pedestrian foot traffic and cars parked at meters along the curbs. Almost every available space was taken.

It was a miracle nobody else was hit.

The car crossed the twenty feet of sidewalk at speed in excess of 100 mph.

People scattered as it suddenly appeared in their midst. It struck the corner of the skyscraper, almost cutting the car in half as it folded its hood around the base of the building. It was better than crashing right through.

The vans followed in the path they had made. They pulled straight onto the pavement in front of the plaza at a relative speed and took up a position covering the entrance. Their intention to be there worked as well as any siren or flashing blue and reds. People kept well back; it looked that official.

Claura and Brother Bucephalus went to check on the Audi driver. Only seconds had passed since their arrival. There was no response from law enforcement yet. Magnus took control of the scene.

He turned by the outer edge of the cordon the vans created. They were parked, sidelong, like a barricade.

"Everybody, stay back!"

He waved them back with both hands high. "It's not safe here! Sir, I'm going to ask you to put the camera phone away."

Jack heard him addressing the crowd that had formed. Things were spiraling rapidly out of control.

It only got worse when the front doors of the plaza began spewing more people.

They were screaming in fear, running for their lives. The level of disorder was threatening to skyrocket.

Brother Vestia was on that side at the front of the lead van. He held his ground, directing the stream to cross the street.

Jack only needed one guess at what caused them to stampede. Then it appeared.

The whole side of the building was sheer glass, polished to a mirror sheen. The Blood Banshee was walking from deep within the reflection, calmly approaching.

"Look!" Jack pointed at it. "There it is!"

Magnus and Claura joined him, and they gathered to rush it.

Henry made his appearance, right behind the fiend. He was in bad shape, but he didn't hesitate as he threw himself at the beast.

The Blood Banshee spun around on him. Grabbing Henry in mid-leap, it continued its turn and whipped him out of the mirror. Henry hit the other three like a bag of cement, and they all went down.

Jack could only watch in horror as the Beast stood before them, one step from the edge of the mirror. It marshaled its strength and raised its yellow eyes to the roof.

2. Just Imagine How Scared Your Friends will be

"Sweet Lord Jesus, NO!" I cried.

The Blood Banshee tipped back its head and roared. It started to bring its claws up in the rapture. It clenched both claws into fists and thrust them towards the ground at its feet. It began to grow.

Up and up and up, its head soared ever upward. Its feet slowly became enormous right before our eyes: twenty-six stories and higher. From our vantage point, it was rising higher than the building itself.

It looked down on us from inside the reflection. We were puny ants, huddled at its feet. The giant monster's toenails breached, from inside, the towering mirror.

Magnus pulled us to our feet before we got stepped on.

"GO, GO, GO!!!" He pushed us, as a group, back into the vans. They pulled away in a squeal of tires, picking up speed before they could be crushed, too.

We remained silent, wrestling with our failure individually.

I looked out the back window in dismay. I had to see for myself. Though I had imagined the possible outcome, the horror of it far outweighed my worst nightmares.

"Fucking great," I complained.

"Now I'm in a Godzilla movie!"

Magnus activated his phone and dialed the Governor's Office.

The Blood Banshee stooped down and emerged from the Gold Building.

Squeezing out, it straightened to its full height. It was five hundred feet tall.

It flexed its gigantic claws like a Japanese horror flick. It roared its deafening call to the sky. Glass exploded from the buildings all around, the sonic destruction affecting an entire city block.

People evacuated the businesses in a sea of human debris. It only served to increase their predicament.

The streets were choked with teaming life. Cars and pedestrians alike were getting in each other's ways. No one was going anywhere. It was utter chaos.

The Giant Beast leered hungrily down on them. Cars were smashed by the dozen, and scores of pedestrians trampled with each step as it waded through the city streets. It scooped up a screaming mass and tossed the doomed people into his mouth.

He chewed a gory mouthful of human beings. Blood ran down his wattled chin.

He had never felt so powerful.

First, he felt what it was like to be an Army. Now he was a Colossus. A colossus of destruction that towered over the rooftops.

He shoved over another skyscraper to watch it topple onto the crowd. Blood ran freely in the streets. It backed up in the gutters.

He looked into top story windows. He smashed his claws into them when he saw incredulous inhabitants. He dragged them out in droves. Whole handfuls of kicking, screaming meat he shoved in his dripping maw. He filled his cheeks.

Nothing on earth possessed the power to stop him now.

"This is Susan James reporting, live, from the Financial District, deep in what is left of, downtown Hartford. I look around at the total destruction of the city's skyline. People have been crushed in groups as they fled to safety."

The reporter choked on her words as bile threatened to rise again. She covered it with the back of her hand as she turned to direct the camera at the flattened remains of a city bus.

"As you can see behind me, this bus has been crushed flat. All of its occupants were trapped inside as a gigantic beast walked through the beleaguered city."

The camera swung back to center on her. The Blood Banshee could, clearly, be seen miles distant. It filled the horizon as it loomed over the skyline.

Backlit by fires, it stalked through geysers of water from broken fire hydrants.

"The fall of Hartford is almost complete as the unknown creature leads its path of destruction. Back to you, Pete."

"We'll bring you more of this breaking news from Susan James in Hartford." the news anchor was saying. A red band of highlights scrolled across the screen beneath him.

The logo of the CBS Channel 3, Action News, was at his back. It no longer felt appropriate to have the city in the background.

"We will continue to bring you, up to the minute, coverage of this tragedy. Once again, a giant monster is rampaging through the streets of Hartford, Connecticut."

"Police are ordering everyone to get into their basements or that everyone seek shelter underground."

"Tornado centers are being opened across the greater New Haven area as everyone is asked to, calmly, move towards safety."

"The Governor's Office is reporting a deployment of the National Guard and the Army Reserves to the area in an emergency effort stop the creature."

"Please stay in your homes." The reporter ordered.

"Once again, a giant monster is storming through downtown Hartford. Take shelter in your basement or seek the nearest tornado shelter."

"This is Peter Anthony. Channel 3 Action News. We'll be back after this short break."

West Hartford, Connecticut
Rosenblatt Army Reserve Center
405th Mobile Artillery Regiment

"Commander Magnus, Special Covert Task Force, sir." The aide de camp was sweating on so many levels. He usually got the blame for any muck ups that occurred during maneuvers. He didn't want to think of what would happen to him now that this had become an impromptu mobilization.

His mistake of ordering twice the amount of artillery shells the opord had called for was not his fault. Those operational orders had so many fragos; he'd lost count.

Mysteriously enough, the fragmentary order that detailed the arrival of the joint vice chief's to view this quarter's proving trials had reached his desk last.

The General about tore him a new one.

Captain Stanford hadn't been aide de camp four months when he started to suspect someone was setting him up for failure. The surplus order of ammo for the howitzers, though, turned out to be an advantage.

When the Vice showed up, he was going to brief them on the mission.

Everyone was glued to the set, watching as Hartford was torn apart. The men were itching for the style of payback only they could offer.

Nothing packed a whollop like the Mobile Artillery. One hundred fifty-five millimeter Howitzers and Patriot Missile systems that fired 410-millimeter rockets were, typically, used to flatten entire sectors from miles away. They had never been used at point-blank range before.

Captain Stanford wished he could be there to see it. He had been bumped to a detail clearing passage from ground zero to someplace called Norwich, only two hours away. Maybe he could make it back in time when things went hot.

Being delegated sure stung. He never gave a thought to the importance of his involvement in saving Hartford. He just wanted to blow that thing up.

Magnus entered the General's office.

"I wanted to thank you, personally, General." He offered his handshake.

"I know." General Hampton said.

"I don't pretend to know who you are or your involvement in this tragedy, Mister. The backing for your request was so high; it burned up on reentry. If you know what I mean."

"That I do, General." Magnus was no stranger to irate officials from other agencies. He preferred to share a moment to smooth things over, particularly in a case like this.

It was urgent they return to Norwich, and they needed transport to bypass traffic. Highway 2 was choked was with evacuees. It didn't hurt to thank the General in person.

"Rest assured, giving us a ride will help end the monster's orgy of destruction. In the meantime, hurt it if you can." He didn't mention his doubts that they would. The best they could do was distract it.

"I understand you had words with the Governor as this was all popping off. We heard a contingent of Raptors are on the way as we speak. That's a whole lot of firepower in a short period of time. I'm impressed, son."

"The Lord provides. General." He nodded to indicate the end of the meeting. He, cooly, made his exit. He had spent more time than he liked on these niceties.

The city burned. He had to go.

He left behind a perplexed officer who turned to his aide.

"Whoever he works for, they sure have their shit together. Are they hiring?" the Captain wondered.

"I don't know." the General retorted. "Are you Catholic?"

I was outside the General's office. Pop was frantic on the other end of the line. I was just trying to keep him calm in hushed tones, hoping nobody would overhear.

"Dad. Calm down. I'm okay."

"You've gotta get outta there, son. You hear me?"

Count on him to be giving orders. Still, I couldn't help feeling touched. I was his only son, after all.

"I'm safe, Pop. We're at the base."

"Have you seen what they're showing on the news?"

"Yeah." I sighed. "I saw it firsthand. We couldn't stop it in time. I watched it. I watched it grow right in front of me. It's gone full-on Godzilla." I must have sounded like I was going into shock. I felt sick to my stomach.

"Get out of there, RIGHT NOW! I want you home safe."

"Yeah. Sure." I was listing fast. The phone was dropping from my lips. Magnus was striding out from the office.

"The Lord provides." he was saying.

He gave me that purposeful look. "Are you ready?" he asked. Always the picture of calm, this one.

"I gotta go, Pop. We're coming back. Don't worry."

And I turned to follow Magnus as we headed out to the landing pad.

Magnus climbed into the waiting helicopter. They rose into the air as he donned an airman's helmet.

He'd had to be sure of the artillery's deployment before he left, or they would have been halfway there by now. Their plan was simple and could save the city. Its' effect would be immediate. Still, He had wanted to ensure some damage was inflicted on that bastard in the meantime.

The artillery was under orders to fire at point-blank range to ensure maximum damage to the Beast.

God save them, Magnus thought. They weren't likely to survive.

He looked down upon the ravaged city. Only rubble remained to inhabit it, strewn with sparking high tension wires.

Jack sat behind him, texting his father.

3. Violence In the Streets

The Blood Banshee stormed over the landscape at a strolling pace. The amount of real estate he demolished with each step was astronomical compared to the effort he expended. He reveled in the dismay it caused. He could see that emotion rise from the ground like a fog.

Purple clouds crackling with bolts of lightning began to form around his knees. Arcs of white-hot plasma raked the ground. The firestorm paraded ahead of his feet, cutting a path in the pavement before him.

He felt invincible. Reaching out, he pulled in great arms full of the racing fear that thickened in hazy streams. He drew them to his giant nostrils and inhaled deeply.

The flood of human adrenaline to his system burned like liquid fire. Every nerve in his enormous body surged with energy.

Sparks danced around his forearms, rising up to his fingertips. His claws glowed with a white corona of sparkling, distilled pain.

He reared back his head and roared like a dragon. The soul fire emerged from his mouth, and a spike of flame began pointing towards the sky. He stood above the city, glowing with incandescent fire fueled by the clouds of mortal suffering. This was more powerful than he ever could have dreamed.

Exultant at the height of five hundred feet, it looked down like a demigod of endless brutality. From the cockpit of a speeding Raptor, it looked like a porcelain lawn ornament tearing up the cabbage patch.

Colonel Frank Rollins, callsign: Fury, made his first pass at five thousand feet. The rest of the F-22 squadrons spread in a V behind him. They came in hot doing Mach 1 as they arrived from the coast. Five flights of seventeen fighters, each, blotted the remaining sunlight like a rug was dropped over the heavens.

They slowed in streamers as the final rank turned in ribbons of impending violence.

The others continued on to turn in their predetermined moments. That way, they stacked a continuous hail storm of rockets to unleash upon the enemy.

The trail fighters aimed themselves directly at the gargantuan beast ravaging the countryside. Increasing their speed, they formed up to take the first attack run.

Heads up displays pinpointed the wretched creature with green triangles of light. The pilots' fingers covered each trigger, awaiting the order.

"Thirty thousand feet. Thirty. We fire at twenty. Three. Two. One. FIRE!"

The Blood Banshee was roaring. Bright flames spilled from his tusked mouth hole.

A blast of flack burst in its face.

Looking down in sudden wrath, he eyed the ranks of toy artillery. Row upon row had served up. Every barrel of the tanklike vehicles, one hundred 155 mm canons, was aimed at it from way down where they sat on their tracks.

"That was just to get your attention." General Hampton chuckled wickedly.

"All guns, prepare to fire on my mark." He barked into his mike. "Fire in sequence by rank. Five-second spread. Keep pouring it on in three. Two. One. FIRE!"

The Blood Banshee barely got both its paws up to shield its face in time. Spitting from the ring of fire at its feet, spikes of black smoke stretched for the beast to end in painful blasts of steel and gunpowder. Chunks of burning shrapnel and flame churned the air in front of him. Crumbling buildings shook in vibrating harmony with the blazing howitzers.

Continuous, deafening, the mass barrage kept going and going. Paws up near its head as it turned to face it away from the shell storm, those yellow phosphorous eyes flashed in sudden anger at the humans' impudence. Its aura came off in a wave of glowing fire as it heaved in a deep breath. The aura burned ever brighter. It built up higher as it channeled its pain, adding it to the power he had reaped from a murdered Hartford. With a roar louder than anything on that battlefield, it released that power in an explosion of concussion force. The shock wave spread out to rock the tracked vehicles back on their shocks. Its roar went on, and the inner fires gleaming from his jaws were stoked by its fury.

It drew in a deep breath. It took in all the air in the surrounding area, vibrated with intensity, and expelled the energetic force to burn the very air. Arcing in a focused beam, the Blood Banshee breathed an all-powerful beam of blue-white plasma flame.

The rockets from the fighter squadrons rammed into its back and proceeded to rain down in droves as their circular flight paths ramped up the flow of concussions and exploding warheads.

The Beast's first blast of overwhelming power had seared three rows of tanks. It had melted them down to slag.

It turned skyward.

It breathed a tight beam at the offending aircraft. The pilots scattered, and some exploded with their craft.

The huge monster bounded forward, plowing the infantry with its gigantic feet into the air. Clearing the rubble of them, he flung them right and left.

The Blood Banshee held his paws up and roared at the world. It glowed stronger and stronger. The roiling fear of a terrified county broadcast by every news network saturated a horrified populace with panic and sorrow. It spread worldwide.

The colossal beast began to grow. Higher and higher, it rose above the heavens. The blazing barrels of the remaining military forces were reduced to firing at one ankle.

Jack Lawrence Sr. received a text message from his son.

"It's from Jack." He held his phone up at the group. "See! He says they're coming back." There was a murmur from the others.

"ETA, ten minutes."

What's this? He thought to himself as he read them from the last bubble.

"Only replaying the record can stop it."

Chapter 5
Satisfaction Guaranteed

405th Air Defense Chopper
50 Feet Above Sea Level
85 Mph

1. Back to Harrow House

The helicopter swept closer to Norwich. Flashing over the rooftops, it scattered everything that was lying loose on the ground with its passage.

Claura had joined the soldiers at the hatch to watch the distant battle. For a second of hope, she dared to believe the military would overtake it. It was lost to view in a pillar of smoke, hammered by the dual attack.

As the scene receded from sight off into the distance, she had seen its hood and cloak lunge forward. A bright beam of light shot from it, and the Beast had aimed it at its enemies.

It still rained fire down on them, turning back and forth, storming forwards to use its feet.

It was obliterating the puny offenders.

She cried out in horror.

"NOOOOOO!" She couldn't tear her eyes off it as it roared at the heavens. In the next moment, its head was rising. It increased in height, doubling its size in seconds.

Stunned, she turned forwards and slumped in her seat.

Jack thumbed furiously at his cell phone. He had to warn his father that they were coming back. He had to get back while Pop was still out of danger. He had tried to reassure his old man that hope wasn't lost.

He realized his father might go ahead and do something foolish.

He hunched over the pilot's shoulder, willing Norwich to come into view.

"At last!" There it was. He turned to grip the rope attached to the hull. He kicked down its end as they slewed to a halt near his roof.

He didn't wait for a word. He slid swiftly to the ground. The impact jarred him as his boots hit.

The others followed, touching down as he sprinted for the front door, yelling.

"Pop!"

He took the stairs in one step and battered through the door. Dashing to the back of the house, he slid into the doorframe and looked, both hands braced, at the stereo in the living room.

2. Each Person in The Room

Norwich, Connecticut
101 North Main Street
Just In The Nick Of Time

Jack Sr. had left the comforts of the military trailer. The priests had gone with his son. There was no one to stop him.

He had a chance to make a difference.

He crept across the snow-covered lawn. He could hear the battle rumbling the air from two hundred miles away. He stepped inside, and the faint whopping sound of a helicopter grew in volume, coming nearer.

His attention was on the interior of the house. Slipping to the back parlor, he spied the stereo. It came on as he closed in.

The record was still on the turntable. The needle was lifted up. The arm moved in towards the record. The needle went down.

Everything fell silent as the scare record began to play. The call of the beast tore out of the speakers. It was the only sound.

Between the howls emitting from the stereo, Jack perked up his ear. The firing had stopped! A smile spread slowly on his lips.

Then there was a crunch, tremendous pain flared in his back, and a claw punched out of his chest. He looked over his shoulder in agonizing defeat.

The Blood Banshee leaned into his face. A look of rage blazed in his eyes. Like floodlights, they burned at the old man's soul.

I got there too late. The Blood Banshee stood over my father, holding him close in a deadly embrace. It pulled his bloody talon out through his back as I leaped for them.

The weight of my dive carried me into my father. I was unable to stop myself. I tackled him to out of the creature's reach.

We lay together on the floor and looked into each other's eyes. He was straining his head to me in an attempt to speak. Blood dripped from the corners of his mouth.

He succeeded in whispering three words.

"I love you…" he said with his dying breath. I held him as his eyes lost focus. They stared beyond my tear-streaked face.

I looked up at the glowing banshee. My eyes narrowed, and I gathered my strength.

The others burst into the room as I launched myself towards it.

"You BASTARD!"

The others joined me in pushing the fiend into the sliding glass door.

We all had our hands on it. The seven of us forced the thing back through the reflection of the sitting room, all the way to the opposite wall.

In its weakened state, it could not shake all of us off. My father had dragged it back through the ether. It had been stripped of its power.

Punches and knees with reinforced plastic hammered into the struggling beast. We took out our combined frustrations in a drum tattoo of smacks and thuds. We were all yelling or screaming our revulsion at its slimy touch.

Henry held up a stake.

The monster struck it from his hand. It thrust its claw under Henry's armored vest.

He went down. Scrabbling around for the stake one-handed, a hammer in the other, his blood poured unchecked. I reached out a hand, sticking my elbow under the creature's neck. We held it tight; it couldn't move.

I yelled to Henry.

"The STAKE!"

"The STAKE!"

"Give me THE STAKE!"

And he did.

I held the point over the monster's black heart. Henry swung down the hammer onto the stake.

Plonk!

Plonk!

Plonk!

Just like in the record. The foul creature's howls rose and, finally, fell.

Henry hammered the stake one last time with the last of his strength.

Plonk!

We held the dying beast until it no longer moved. Stepping back, we watched its head slip down. Its chin rested on its chest.

We staggered, holding each other up as we fell out of the mirror. In a pile of panting bodies, we eased back onto the floor. I took my father into my lap as Claura held Henry. The pool of his life's blood pushed outwards beneath them. The scars on her left forearm faded completely.

He looked up at the frost blue angel that rocked him so gently. Claura sniffed as he stared her firmly in the eye.

"Its days of evil are over," he said.

"The Blood Banshee is dead! Uuuuuugh."

2. Six Months Later
Norwich, Connecticut
101 North Main Street
April 1st, 2019

The story had met its end with the destruction of the Blood Banshee. They had kept watching it where it was pinned in the reflection.

It began to fade. It was, soon, lost from sight. Only the wooden stake protruding from the wall was the lasting evidence it had ever hung there.

The stake was left in the wall in the mortal realm. It stays there to this day.

Claura was three months pregnant. They had tied the knot the day after New Year's. Jack had proposed, down on one knee, in the ten seconds the Ball had dropped.

Their future was bright. Claura's report had been exclusive. Sales of the Cryptic Times shot through the roof.

Demand for the issue showcasing the Gayle House Haunting and the Blood Banshee forced them to close for an entire week. That was the time it took to run three extra printings. The public wasn't satisfied until she had written the book.

Scare Record topped the New York Times Bestseller List in one short hour.

Jack was taking to his role as a loving husband. He assumed full responsibility for the tenants at Harrow House.

They hailed him as a hero—every day.

Magnus showed up for the nuptials. He whisked them away for an extended; all-expense paid, honeymoon in Rome. On the third day, they had been called in for a briefing. It was brief.

Cardinal Commander John Culpiscacia preceded them into the presence of the Pope. He apologized sincerely for detaining them further. He wanted to thank them for their assistance and, fervently, bless them.

They had returned to Norwich only last week.

Jack and Claura stood in the bay window wrapping an arm around one another, interlinked. They shared an unspoken bond. They both could tell what the other was thinking all the time.

He placed his free hand on Claura's belly and baby Henry.

Epilogue

Devonshire, England
Bearnes, Hampton & Littlewood
Exeter, United Kingdom
March 31st, 2025

"The Bidding is closed." The lilting voice of the auctioneers carried softly over the crowd.

In the well-lit hall, the fountain statue of the Goddess Diana was removed from in front of the podium. Two men held it steady on the pallet as the pallet jack operator raised it up and moved it smoothly out.

"Next, for the horror fans…" he chortled, "Is this one of a kind piece." A gentleman in livery came to his side. He handed the speaker a small shipping envelope.

Picking the package up from the page's fingertips without looking, he surveyed the crowd with a severe expression.

Sliding out the contents into his waiting right hand, he flourished it up for the room.

"It is the First Original Master of the Gayle House Haunting." The collective intake of breath from the crowd rocked to and fro among the gathering. Then all were silent.

"Legend has it, the spirit of Bloody Mary was bonded to the vinyl by its call at the very moment of its recording."

"Danger level *is* high. Bidding will begin at a quarter of a million pounds."

The fearful hush remained about the auction house. Noone dared move a muscle.

"Any takers? A quarter of a million. No takers. The amount at the start of bidding is firm—one-quarter of a million pounds."

"Ah. The man in the corner will see it at a quarter of a million. Going once."

He paused.

"Going twice." No one else moved a paddle.

"Congratulations, Sir. You are now the owner of the First Original Master of the Gayle House Haunting. Are you prepared to take responsibility of the item?"

The crooked man raised his paddle in ascent. He slung himself to his feet and hobbled up to the podium. Signing a receipt, he crooked his nose to look in avarice at his prize.

Won't his nephews be surprised! The last Lords of Waverley liked their American comic books. He wasn't waiting for his two wards to misspend his rightful inheritance.